E.J.Kay is the pen name of Liz Falconer. Born in Bolton, Lancashire, Liz is now a professor at a university in the South West of England. She specializes in the use of technology to enhance learning in higher education, but has had a lifelong interest in archaeology and theories of human evolution. She lives with her husband and son in the beautiful and historic county of Wiltshire. Her website is at www.ejkay.com.

Watermark

E.J.Kay

Anniversary Press

Copyright © E.J.Kay 2012
The author asserts the moral right to be identified as the author of this book.

Published by Anniversary Press, Calne, Wiltshire, U.K.
www.anniversarypress.co.uk

ISBN: 978-0-9572078-3-7

Print edition
2nd edition

Anniversary Press is a trading name granted under license to Anniversary Software Services Ltd.

Dedications

This book is dedicated to Elaine Morgan, whose intelligence, bravery, generosity and determination are an inspiration to us all.

Also to my wonderful husband and beautiful son. My own, personal inspirations.

Author's note

Whilst Watermark is a work of fiction, the archaeological, historical, scientific and religious references are factual. The bibliography includes the major sources used in the book, together with suggestions for further reading. Through the medium of the fictional story the book explores some of the current thinking in the study of human evolution, focussing on the role played by water and what has become known as the 'aquatic ape hypothesis'. But, if you're not interested in the puzzles of evolution, there is still a whodunit puzzle to solve!

The aquatic ape hypothesis, or AAH, is the idea that ancestors of modern humans spent a significant amount of time in aquatic environments, and that our physiology has at least partly been shaped by adapting to living in, or very near, water. Like most hypotheses it has its strong proponents and equally strong antagonists. And some people have no time for evolution as a theory in any case, whatever the environmental arguments.

One thing seems to be clear, though. As a species we have an amazing ability to believe in things! The world can be interpreted in so many different ways. And that has always interested me. Our personalities; our experiences; our fears; our need to belong to our family, clan or identifying group: all of these seem to influence how we see the world and the evidence we choose to believe as "true".

Personally, I love uncertainty. Because that's when we get to ask the most interesting questions.

And sometimes an idea can just capture our imaginations.

1

She took in a deep breath and held it, then dived under the clear blue surface of the lake. She was good at this, the best in her group. All of the group could swim well but only a few could dive, and they only managed to stay under the water for a few seconds before they had to come up, coughing and spluttering. She could stay down long enough to gather the shellfish that clung to the rocks on the sandy floor of the lake. This was her task for today. Striking out for the bottom she saw the bed of freshwater mussels on the rocks below her, smooth and inviting as they caught the sunlight reflected from the surface ripples. Prizing the shells off the rocks was easy now that she had learned to take a small stone chip down with her. Picking up the shells, she held as many as she could in her long curved fingers and kicked back up towards the air. As her head broke the surface she saw the sparkling water stretching away into the distance, the islands rising hazily out of the lake. She turned over onto her back and headed for the nearby shore, kicking her legs whilst holding the shells against her body with her hands. When she reached shallow water she stood up and waded ashore.

She was quite tall for her sex; around five feet eight inches. The covering of fine hair that whorled around her breasts and pointed up towards her muscular shoulders was so short that the sun glistened on the dark, wet skin beneath. Her long legs were covered with fine hair too, and her sturdy, densely-muscled thighs rippled with every footfall as she waded ashore; strong legs and springy feet made walking on the wet sand easy. Her mouth jutted outwards from a heart-shaped face under pronounced brow ridges that helped to shield her eyes from the strong sunlight. There was little hair on her face, apart from thick eyebrows and a light covering on her top lip and chin. Thick, short, black hair covered the top and back of her head, where it joined the finer hair of her neck.

Many of her group were wading in the shallows and when they saw her coming back they chattered excitedly. Clicking, lip-smacking and making short, staccato vocalisations that meant "good food", they ran towards her, splashing through the water. Shellfish were a favourite meal for the group, a real delicacy, and her ability to gather them gave her a status in the group that was higher than the other females. And many of the males. The group lived almost exclusively on fish and other aquatic animals, including the small helmeted turtles that swam in the lake. There were few other animals on any of the islands, even though many of them were large and all of them covered in rich grass and brush. There were only a few trees left now, but the shrubby plants and grasses were varied and provided a good supply of fruit, roots and vegetation. But it was water that dominated their lives. As she turned and waded back towards the deeper water to collect more shellfish, the group gathered around to prize open this latest catch with stone flake scrapers and put them on the pile of food they had prepared for the evening meal. On a high rock nearby the sentinels kept watch for signs of crocodiles, but today they didn't seem to be interested and had stayed away from the group's favourite fishing grounds.

The alpha male sat some distance away from the main group. He watched her swim out to the shellfish beds and dive down again, coming up soon afterwards with another large handful of shells. Squinting into the sunlight he chewed the ends of his fingers. His legs were a couple of inches longer than hers and he was covered in more hair too, although it was still fine and his skin showed through clearly. He was a good swimmer with his head above the water and he frequently swam over to neighbouring islands to hunt turtle and large fish. But, he could not dive. He had tried and tried, watching the diving female to see how she did it, but as soon as his head was underwater he would choke and splutter and have to surface quickly. When he asked her how she did it, pointing to the deeper water and making the 'how?' sound, she had said "here" and pointed to the back of her throat. To be truthful, she didn't really know how she did it, and certainly didn't have the words to explain. So, all he could do was watch her dive with a growing feeling of frustration grinding in his gut.

The diving female waded out to where the water came up to her waist, kicked out with an easy, strong swimming stroke, and then dived down towards the shellfish beds again. She loved this; the sense of freedom, the feeling of being an important part of the group. The clear water made seeing the shellfish bed easy, and she chose the big shells that had juicy meat inside them. She prized them off the rocks and kicked back up to the surface. Once she was back at the shore, the group picked up their scrapers again and set about releasing the flesh from the shells. At the meal that evening they had a feast of fish, shellfish, roots and fruit, roasted over the open fire. The alpha male ate his share of shellfish too, his hunger overcoming his jealousy.

In the late evening the group became quiet, all having eaten their fill, and as the sun set over the lake they sat with their backs to the land, sleepily gazing out across the water. But the alpha male didn't relax. He couldn't. He lay on his back in the crook of a bush, with a picture of the diving female lodged in his mind. Until recently he had admired her ability to dive so well, but lately he found it was making him more and more angry. He had become the dominant male just the year before, following on from his father who had died suddenly. Although he was quite young to be an alpha at just eighteen years old, his status still conferred the right for a small harem and he had readily exercised that right, choosing three mates from the group. Other males were also allowed to mate and couples were faithful and monogamous. Well, most of the time. The diving female was paired with another male and as such he shouldn't touch her. But he didn't really want to mate with her anyway. He wanted to kill her. Even though she helped to feed the group, and the group's wellbeing was his responsibility, he simply could not overcome his growing jealousy of her. She was challenging his status; making him look smaller by making herself look bigger. Not acceptable. Something would have to be done.

In the late afternoon next day he sat on a low rock, knapping a stone. He was good at making tools this way, and it was partly due to this ability that the group had accepted his status as alpha at such a young age. Some of the stone shards he made were very sharp, and the group used them to cut the flesh of turtles out of their shells. Today he was making a large hand axe; a very useful tool for chopping through wood and brush. And hitting the diving female hard on the head. Part of him knew he should not be thinking this, and part of him knew how much he wanted to do it. The familiar knotting in his stomach returned. He wrinkled his brow, his protruding brow ridge accentuating the line above his eyes, partly from concentration but mostly from anger and frustration. He would do it tonight. Make an end of it. Give himself some peace.

Twilight came as the diving female sat with her back to the shore of the lake, gazing out across the water. Her mate and their two children had gone back to the night rest site with the rest of the group, but she remained at the water's edge alone, drinking in the last of the sunset. The alpha male approached from behind, slowly and quietly. Now was his chance. Twilight doesn't last long in tropical Africa; he would have to make his move quickly. There was still enough light to see by, but only just. As he got near her she heard him and turned around. At first she raised her eyebrows and smiled in greeting, but when she saw the look on his face she knew she was in trouble. She jumped up and instinctively ran towards the water as fast as she could. But he was too fast for her. He caught up with her before she could reach the water, grabbed hold of her arm and pulled her round towards him, raising the axe in his right hand. He brought it down on the back of her head with a crunching thud, burying the point into the base of her skull. She hardly made a noise, just a low moan, and slumped in his arms. He dropped her, and the axe, and ran back to the undergrowth, resisting the temptation to look behind him. His heart was pounding with exhilaration; he almost beat his chest, but then remembered that this was not an action he wanted share with the rest of the group. He crouched down behind a bush and watched her.

She pulled herself up on her arms and saw the axe in front of her. Picking it up she crawled to the edge of the lake where she managed to stand up and wade out a little. The back of her head burned and ached and she yearned to get into the water to take the pain away. She would give the axe to the lake as an offering, in return for its help. Groggily she swam out towards her favourite shellfish beds, the blood that trailed out behind her leaving a scarlet streak in the gently rippling water. As she looked out over the lake to the deep red sky where the sun had set, she let the axe fall from her hand; it sank and hit the sandy bottom, raising a cloud around it. The islands became fuzzy and indistinct as she began to lose consciousness; she blacked out and slipped under the surface, the air escaping from her lungs in small bubbles as her body sank down to the shellfish beds and draped, face down, over one of the rocks. As a gentle underwater current lifted her feet slightly, they caught under the edge of the rock. The last remaining bubbles of her breath rose slowly, leaving her at peace at the bottom of the lake.

2

Joseph stepped out of the shower and leaned over to pull a towel off the rail.

"Mm, mm," called his wife from the bed, with a wolf-whistle intonation. He bowed jokingly, his shoulder-length hair falling forward over his face, and then carried on drying himself, smiling. He was a good-looking man, tall and light-skinned, and although he had turned fifty the previous September he still had a lean body and an athletic build. He held the good Irish family name of Connor; as clear a testament to his Celtic roots as his black hair and sapphire eyes.

"So, Alec is back tomorrow then?" asked Anna.

"Yes, together with his new girlfriend. She's a little older than him. About one and a half million years. And dead. His perfect partner." Joseph hung the towel back on the rail, closed the bathroom door and fell onto the bed. "I foresee a long and happy relationship, unlike the ones he's had with live women."

"Aw, poor Alec, he can't help how he is. And you know you always stick up for him in the end."

Joseph yawned. "Yes, I do. He's a good man with a good brain. I don't think he'd survive anywhere other than a university though. He just has no idea how to deal with people. I'm amazed he managed to talk the Kenyan authorities into allowing him to bring the remains back with him. I must admit I'm glad he did though. I can't wait to take a look at them myself."

"Old bones," teased Anna, stretching lazily. "What are they good for?"

Joseph put his arms around his wife's waist and pulled her tight against his damp skin, making her giggle. "I'll show you what old bones are good for," he whispered.

Mike Osewe stood at the office window, gazing out across the grey, wet city to the Irish Sea in the distance. The University of the North West of England's archaeology and palaeontology department was housed in an old building that had started out as a mental hospital in the 1870's. The rooms all had high ceilings and the corridor walls were still covered with dark green ceramic tiles from the floor to the wooden dado rail, topped off with the characteristic cream tiles that were all the rage in Victorian institutional buildings. The long corridors were lined with thick wooden doors under frosted glass transom lights and, despite attempts to brighten up the walls with maps and pictures, the gloomy atmosphere of illness and institution still hung in the air.

A light knock came at Mike's office door; he shouted "hello" just as it opened. A smart, short-haired female head wearing designer glasses peered in.

"Ah, Mike, is Joseph about?"

"No, he's teaching just now, but he should be back in about ten minutes. Do you want me to ask him to see you?"

"Oh, yes please. I'll be in my office for the next hour or so." Professor Juliet Bailey, Dean of the Faculty of Science, pulled the door closed behind her.

Mike wrote a note on Joseph's desk pad in case he forgot to give him the message and found himself wondering for the umpteenth time why Juliet used email so infrequently. She always seemed to prefer to walk around the corridors to make contact. It was a good habit, he supposed, as it made her visible in the faculty, and she did have a particular interest in the department of archaeology and palaeontology. Although she spent a significant part of her time managing the faculty of science, she was still an archaeologist of considerable distinction herself.

He returned to his position at the window to watch the steady rain cascade across the mottled slate roof of the town hall. When Joseph came back into the office fifteen minutes later, Mike was still lost in thought. He jumped as Joseph put his books down on the desk. "Oh, hi. Er, Juliet wants to see you," he said.

"What, now?"

"In your own time, as long as that's in the next forty minutes!"

"Did she say what it was about?"

Mike shook his head and returned to his window vigil. "Nope."

"You OK?"

Mike turned round again. "Yeah, I'm fine. Look, I'll tell you when you get back from your meeting with Juliet. It's no big deal, honestly."

"Hopefully I won't be long. But you know what Juliet can be like."

The office door was closed when Joseph got there, so he went round to her PA's office.

"Hi Mary," he said. "Juliet wanted to see me. Her door's closed so I guess she's busy?"

"She's just on the phone, she won't be a minute. Take a seat. I'll let her know you're here when she's finished her call."

Juliet's office was part of the Faculty Executive suite and had a door leading directly out onto the corridor, as well as one that lead through to the central office shared by the two PAs who looked after the dean, the two associate deans and the faculty administrator. Her executive colleagues always kept their corridor doors closed, forcing any visitors to enter through this central office. But Juliet deliberately kept her corridor door open if she weren't busy. The faculty was large and sprawling and the previous dean had been very distant. Juliet was determined to have an accessible and open feel to her deanship.

Joseph sat down next to a large glass case that contained a collection of archaeological remains. Of particular value and interest in this display was a Bronze Age sword that had been discovered in an excavation at Flag Fen in Cambridgeshire. It was an elegant elongated teardrop shape that came to a sharp point and had clearly been a valuable item in its own time. The mud of the fen had preserved it in remarkable condition, and it showed how later Bronze Age craftsmen had extended the blade of a sword to form a tang that would have been the basis for a handle. Making the handle part of the blade made the sword much stronger and less likely to break; points of attachment are points of weakness. Making an offering to the water must have been an exceptionally important act for someone to give up a sword as precious as this. It had been ritually presented to the water by the side of a wooden causeway that had been constructed across marshland around three thousand five hundred years ago. The sword had been excavated from the fen during an English Heritage dig in the mid-1980s and ritually presented once again; this time to the University of the North West of England on receiving its charter in 1992. Joseph had taken part in the Flag Fen explorations as part of his research at Birmingham University, working on his PhD in paleobiology, and he always looked at the sword with great fondness whenever he came to the executive office.

Mary stirred him from his thoughts and ushered him into Juliet's office. It wasn't particularly spacious, considering she was the dean of the faculty. It was a bit of a squeeze to fit her desk, a meeting table and five chairs in the same room as all her bookshelves and travel mementos. Plaster casts of ancient primate skulls had pride of place in a glass cabinet, together with stone hand axes and flint arrowheads, and the walls of her office were hung with photographs going back more than twenty years. Some were of her in shorts and T-shirts, kneeling in dusty holes. Others were of smarter occasions; international conferences and foreign government seminars.

"Thanks for coming, Joseph. Please do have a seat. So," she said, leaning forward to rest her elbows on the desk and steeple her slender hands, "Alec returns this afternoon. It's going to be quite an occasion. I expect the press to be out in some force at the airport."

"It's going to be a great day for him, and for the university too, don't you think?" Joseph replied.

Juliet leaned back, her hands still steepled. "I think what he has achieved is remarkable. The most complete and best preserved hominin remains ever found." She paused. "And in such an interesting context."

Ah, here it comes, he thought.

"He is, of course, very excited about the location of the remains," Juliet continued. "As he favours the hypothesis that water played such an important role in human evolution, it's clearly a highly relevant find for him. But I think that we need to be careful about jumping to any sudden conclusions, particularly when it comes to handling the popular press."

Joseph liked Juliet, but she certainly could be pompous at times. "I thought he came over very well on his Radio Four interview," he said, with a wry smile. "It sounded quite measured, for Alec. Although perhaps the poor telephone link to Kenya helped to take the edge off his voice."

Juliet became more agitated. "Yes, well, he's less measured on his blog. I have also been interviewed by the press whilst Alec has been on the excavation, and it was very difficult to achieve the necessary balance. I want to support Alec, and to help the university to make the most of this find, but I cannot outwardly support what many scientists in the field, including myself, still consider to be a crackpot theory. Although I largely trust the Guardian, as far as I trust any newspaper, they clearly wanted to play up the 'theory proved' angle. This is serious Joseph. Our research funding comes to us in direct proportion to our reputation and some of

Alec's blog postings have been making what amount to claims of proof of the aquatic ape hypothesis."

"He does sometimes get carried away," agreed Joseph. "I don't think he really considers the readers of his blog – he sees it as more of a personal diary. But then he never considers anyone else anyway. Other people aren't Alec's strong suit. But, sorry Juliet, what do you want me to do about this?"

"You are one of the few people Alec listens to. I know you've known each other for some time and that he was your student at Birmingham. Alec followed you here to UNWE too, so it's clear he values your friendship. I'm just asking you to try to get him to see that we need to proceed carefully here. For everyone's good."

Particularly for your good, thought Joseph. "I'll have a discreet word with him and see if I can get him to understand."

"He had better understand, or things will not go well for him!"

Juliet was more agitated than Joseph had ever seen her before. He found it disconcerting and made a move to get up. "OK, I'll have a word with him. Sorry, but I need to get back to prep for my tutorial group. I've got them this afternoon before Alec arrives. Your preparations for the welcome party are going OK?"

She regained some of her composure. "Yes, thank you. I have the greatest respect for Alec's archaeological abilities, you know. I'll be very happy to see him back safely with us."

When Joseph returned to the office he shared with Mike, he clicked the kettle on and put tea bags into a couple of grimy mugs. "You look rattled, what happened?" Mike asked.

"Juliet's going ape about Alec and his water baby."

"Going ape, ha ha," said Mike, and then he caught Joseph's expression. "Ah, you're serious."

"I've never seen her like this before. OK, they've had professional fall-outs over human evolutionary theories before now, but Juliet seems really angry this time. She says it's because of the reputational damage that could be done to the university, but I'm not so sure. I actually think she might be worried that Alec has something here that could discredit her. Or at least discredit her refusal to entertain any human evolutionary theory that depends on water as an environmental pressure for selection."

"High stakes, then."

"Mmm."

Mike made the tea in silence, while Joseph took up his space at the window. There was something about looking out over the city, away to the grey sea in the distance, which helped both of them to think more clearly.

"Oh hey, sorry. You were going to tell me the cause of your current distraction," said Joseph, turning round just in time to receive a scalding hot cup of tea.

"Sophie's pregnant." A bald statement.

Joseph grinned from ear to ear. "Oh fantastic news, congratulations!"

"Thanks, yeah, we're really looking forward to the baby." Joseph caught the downbeat in Mike's answer.

"But?"

"No buts, really!"

Silence.

"OK, to be honest it's all freaking me out. It's not the baby or the responsibility, or Sophie. I love her to bits. It's just how things are changing. Thirtieth birthday last year, now I'm going to be a dad. Bloody hell!"

"Y'know, when Anna got pregnant with Mark and Jenny we both felt exactly the same way. In fact, I think it hit Anna harder than me. Course, we had the double whammy of finding out it was twins!"

"I think Sophie's feeling it too, not least because she's feeling so lousy. She's got no energy to do anything and feels sick almost all the time. It's a real bummer for her. And I just feel like a complete spare part."

"When's she due?"

"Early September."

Joseph grinned again. "Good time to be born. Seriously though, talk to her about this."

Mike looked doubtful. "I don't want to give her anything else to worry about while she feels so lousy. I'm just having a thirty-something wobble. I'll be OK."

Joseph smiled at his colleague and then caught sight of the clock on the wall behind him. "Oh hell, I've got that tutorial group in an hour. I'd better think of something to say to them. And I need a sandwich." *Actually,* he thought, *after a morning like this I need a stiff drink.*

3

The doorbell rang repeatedly.

"OK, I'm coming. For Christ's sake, gimme a break." The thin young woman walked quickly down the hallway and opened the door. "Where's the fuckin' fire?!" The hooded figure pushed her back down the hallway and held her hard against the wall. "OK, OK, take it easy. Like it rough d'ya? That's OK, I can do rough. No need for anyone to get hurt."

"You stay away from Alec Whickham," the figure rasped in a deep voice. "Skanky whore." The intruder held her tight by the arms and then suddenly turned her round with one arm up her back. "This is a warning you shouldn't ignore." Her attacker pushed her against the wall again, this time making her hit her head against the kitchen door frame; then she was suddenly let go and the hooded figure ran back down the hall and out of the house.

She propped herself up against the wall for a moment, trying to control how much she was shaking. Then she ran towards the front door, closed and locked it and put on the security chain. Walking back to the kitchen she picked up a packet of cigarettes from the hall table, took one out and put it in her mouth; her hand was still trembling. The livid red marks on her arms were already beginning to show signs of bruising as she searched for matches in the drawer under the sink.

"Come on, come on. Must have some somewhere. Oh, thank God." The match sputtered into life. She lit the cigarette and drew a deep breath of comforting smoke. *I've got to get out of this game*, she thought to herself.

4

Doctor Alec Whickham was already fastening his seatbelt as the steward's voice came over the address system. "Ladies and gentlemen, we're about to begin our descent into Manchester Airport. Please fasten your seat belts and make sure ...."

Alec's thoughts drifted as the plane banked to the left and he could see the Derbyshire hills beneath them. Everything was so green. After four months in Africa the English countryside looked like a different planet. His research student, Egraine Mountford, and his post-doctoral research associates Ben Magnusson and Lily White (whose parents either had a wicked sense of humour or none at all) were chatting about the first things they were going to do after they landed and the hoo-ha of the welcome back was over.

"OK, so, in order of priority; get laid, go to Pizza Hut, watch the Simpsons, phone my mum and dad, get rat-arsed."

"Honestly Ben, I don't know how your girlfriend puts up with you. Are you at least intending to say hello to her before dragging her off to bed?" asked Lily in exasperation. Four months of Ben's macho sense of humour had stretched her patience to breaking point.

"At least he left getting drunk till last," said Egraine. "She'll be grateful for that."

"I think it would be appropriate to get into a more academic frame of mind," said Alec over his shoulder.

"Sorry Alec." Ben looked a little sheepish. "It's just really exciting. I still can't actually believe what's in the hold of this plane. And, even more, that I'm a part of it."

Alec smiled a flat, humourless smile. The truth was that he couldn't quite believe it either. Finally, exoneration. After years of battling against academic conservatism and colleagues promoting themselves rather than the subject under study, this was the evidence he had been looking for. He couldn't be ignored now. *Even Juliet would have to concede this one.*

Born and brought up in Newcastle on the North East coast of England and the youngest of three brothers, Alec had been an introverted and quiet child. His parents had hoped that he would become more sociable as he got older, but that had never happened. His bedroom had been full of dinosaur pictures and models, wall charts showing the development of Homo sapiens and books devoted to palaeontology and archaeology. The few friends he brought home from school didn't usually come back more than once, apparently unsettled by the intensity of Alec's interests and his complete lack of empathy. He did have one closer friend, Robbie, who shared his interest in fossils, but even he was a fairly occasional visitor. Alec's favourite family holidays had been to the south coast of England, along the Jurassic Coast around Lyme Regis and Charmouth, and all he ever wanted to do was to walk the beaches collecting fossils.

His interests had developed and focused as he got older. A natural scientist, his marks were always high in school and he left with four 'A' grade A levels, going on to study archaeology and palaeontology at Manchester University and then to research his PhD at Birmingham, investigating the environments that may have contributed to early human development. Birmingham was where Alec had first met the aquatic ape hypothesis, or AAH. Browsing through a bookshop in the Bull Ring one weekend, he had come across a book titled 'The Scars of Evolution' by Elaine Morgan. The title immediately caught his interest, so he bought a copy. As he began to read it the arguments truly fascinated him. He had always struggled to reconcile existing theories of human evolution with the things that make humans human. Grasslands habitats just didn't add up as being the environmental context for human development. Bipedalism, functional hairlessness, increased fat, breathing control, copious sweating, high dependence on water and large brain development is a collection of adaptations that, in combination, are unique to humans. Alec had always believed that the environment that promoted selection for these was likely to be peculiar to humans too. Otherwise, why are there no other walking, talking apes? Why just us? And why are we so different from our surviving ape relatives? Elaine Morgan's book argued that the major environmental pressure that resulted in the evolution of humans was water. Not just a quick wade through a stream every now and again, but a long and close relationship with it that resulted in the development of characteristics that are more commonly seen in aquatic mammals.

It only took Alec an afternoon and evening to read the book, but it changed his life. He had been struggling to find a topic for his doctoral research, and that afternoon it suddenly became clear; the characteristics that make us human are recognisable aquatic adaptations. He immediately determined that his thesis would add to the body of knowledge that supported this view. However, the AAH was far from popular with the mainstream view of human evolution, and he encountered considerable resistance to researching the topic for his PhD. The research committee that considered his application initially rejected it, saying that the AAH was neither provable nor falsifiable, and as such was not a suitable subject for doctoral research. Alec didn't give up, though. Alec never gave up. But he would have been unlikely to succeed if he hadn't had the good fortune to be introduced to Joseph Connor, then a senior lecturer in paleobiology, as a potential tutor. Joseph quickly recognised Alec's intellect and that, despite his very apparent social difficulties, he was capable of ground-breaking research. In a characteristic act of open-mindedness, Joseph agreed to help Alec to formulate his research proposal and then to supervise him, a task he later described as both exhilarating and frustrating in equal measure. In the end, Alec's PhD put together a persuasive enough theoretical test of the hypothesis to achieve his doctorate. But that didn't mean that Joseph was totally persuaded by the AAH. Or that many other specialists in the field were either.

As the plane made its final approach into Manchester Airport Alec thought back to the day he first saw the tell-tale edge of ancient bone protruding from the ground on the eastern shore of Lake Turkana. As they began to scrape and brush away the surrounding earth, the extent of the preservation became clearer hour by hour. Most of the long bones in the legs and arms had remained intact, but the ribs were broken into a number of pieces that would need to be reconstructed. The pelvis was also broken, but only in three places, and the pubic arch was intact enough to identify the remains as most likely to be female. The skull was in fifteen pieces, but it did appear that most of it was present. It promised to be quite a jigsaw puzzle. The position of the bones suggested that the final resting position of the animal's body had been draped over a rock that had fossilised fresh water mussels attached to it, with a hand axe lying close by. The skeleton was face down, set into the sediment, and some parts were stuck firmly to the rock beneath. Alec had decided that the best method was to dig under the remains and the rock and try to lift it all as one, with the sediment base intact. This had been both fiddly and heavy work, but they had managed to do it successfully and crate it up safely. He had also succeeded in getting the Kenyan authorities to agree to him bringing the finds back to the UK for investigation, although he only had them for four months so he and his team would have to proceed quickly. But, they also needed to undertake the cleaning carefully, measuring and accurately dating the skeleton together with the fossilised shellfish and the hand axe.

He was sure that the hominin remains and the shellfish would be contemporaneous, which would mean that the creature whose skeleton it was had died in the water. Not by water, but actually in it. Not proof that human ancestors went through a totally aquatic phase, but persuasive that the water was an environment that was in close proximity to developing Homo species. *As if that needed proving through the fossil record,* he thought. *How could an animal that sweats and drinks as much as humans do have evolved anywhere else than in an environment that had plenty of fresh water? Particularly somewhere as hot as Africa. How many times have I endured reading the hypothesis that sweating developed as a response to living in a hot and dry environment? Absolute nonsense.*

Alec was roused from his contemplations by the plane landing with a bump on the runway. It taxied towards its nominated gate, drew to a halt, and Alec and his small party undid their seatbelts and started to get their belongings from the overhead lockers. As the door opened a cold March breeze blew into the cabin, reminding them that they had definitely left Africa. It had been another very cold winter in the UK and the wind still carried an icy edge. Lily shivered and pulled on her jumper. Outside the plane the cargo doors were already being opened and the crate containing the fossilised remains was unloaded by scissor lift. Once they had passed through customs Alec and his team found a small group of journalists waiting in the arrivals lounge; the regional BBC science correspondent and a couple of journalists from the local press. Not the mob that Juliet had expected. They answered the journalists' questions as patiently as they could and then made their excuses and squeezed themselves into the cabin of the waiting UNWE van, with its precious cargo in the rear. Alec and Ben sat in the front, while Lily and Egraine belted themselves into the seats behind.

"Typical," said Lily. "Men in front, women behind."

"Yeah, great. They're first through the windscreen," said Egraine and Lily laughed. "Anyway, I've been thinking. Maybe we should give the find a name. It doesn't seem right to just keep calling her 'it'. Don Johansson called his Australopithecine 'Lucy'. I've got an idea for a name for our find."

"What?" asked Lily.

"Well, I think we should call her Nimue[1] . She was the Lady of the Lake in Le Morte d'Arthur."

"Oh I love it!" squeaked Lily. "The lady of the lake. Perfect!"

"What do you think Alec?" asked Egraine, leaning forward and brushing her mouth close to his ear.

Alec moved his head away. "Yes, why not. Better than letting the press decide."

Egraine smiled. "Ben?"

"Not bothered."

Lily and Egraine looked at each other and rolled their eyes. "Nimue it is," they both said together.

The university had organised a civic reception, including the Mayor, the Lord High Sheriff, the Chancellor of the University and the senior management team, together with other local dignitaries and representatives from the press. The reception had been organised in the staff restaurant

---

[1] Pronounced Nim-oo-ay

for three o'clock that afternoon, as Alec and his party of four (including Nimue) were due back around that time. Things had run pretty much to time, so at three-thirty pm the van arrived at the university, pulling into the loading bay in the underpass between the science building and the gym. Alec set about supervising the unloading until Ben reminded him that they were supposed to go up to the reception. Very reluctantly Alec left the unloading and went up to the refectory with his three research colleagues, but by this time it was past four o'clock.

Juliet was clearly irritated by the time he got there. She was annoyed that the party had been left waiting until after four for no good reason. She put a brave face on it and accompanied Alec whilst he was interviewed by the attending journalists, but at the first opportunity she took him over to one side.

"Alec, what took so long? When we spoke on the phone at three fifteen you said about ten minutes. We have some very important guests here."

"I needed to be sure that the remains were properly handled. That's much more important than attending some publicity stunt, Juliet. It was always going to be risky to organise something today, but you would insist on going for dramatic effect. If you think about what could have gone wrong I think the timing worked out OK." Alec turned away and headed over to chat to Joseph, leaving Juliet fuming.

"What was that about?" asked Joseph. "Juliet doesn't look too happy."

"Oh, she's annoyed at us being late for this bash. I mean, really, what does that matter in comparison to what I've brought back here? To tell the truth, I think she's pissed at me because she's actually worried about what this find could mean for her reputation."

"Mm, actually, I need to have a quick word with you about that. Juliet asked me to talk to you to make sure that you don't make any unwarranted claims about the relevance of this find to the AAH. She's concerned about the effect it may have on the university's mainstream position and the funding we receive."

"I thought you were sympathetic."

"Oh come on Alec, you've known me long enough to know my position on this. I think there are some interesting aspects to the AAH, but I have major issues with the timelines. Bipedalism and hair loss happened millions of years apart, from the best evidence we have, so I struggle with the idea that a single environmental change brought about everything that makes us human."

"The hair loss evidence is genetic," snorted Alec.

"But it's still reputable evidence, Alec. Remember our tutorial discussions all those years ago about the importance of keeping an open mind in research? Archaeology suggests that bipedalism was around at least four million years ago, if not earlier. Genetics suggests that we lost our hair a couple of million years later. They are two pieces of evidence that are hard to reconcile with a single environmental event that led to the development of our most human characteristics."

"The answer will lie with archaeology, I'm sure of it. There's a lot more interpretation, and downright guesswork, than anyone would like to own up to in genetics. But bones are bones and can be dated pretty reliably, if they're found in the right condition and in the right place."

"But bones are also open to a lot of interpretation too Alec, you know that. And they tell a limited story. You have to be very lucky to find anything ancient that has hair or soft tissue evidence."

"The Darwinius remains from the Messel Pit[2] prove that it can be done though. And they're more than forty million years old. For early Homo species we only need to go back two to three million years."

"Yes," admitted Joseph, "that's true. But the Messel Pit is a very peculiar environment. You're not likely to find anything with hair outlines and identifiable stomach contents in the African Rift Valley. Anyway, look, we're going over old ground here. I'm just asking you to please be circumspect in your comments about the find."

"So that Juliet can relax?"

"Well, yes, in a nutshell. She does also have legitimate concerns about funding streams. You know I'm not saying that you shouldn't publicise your findings. I am on your side, believe it or not. We all know that the internet has led to information being available about our work much earlier than it

[2] The Messel Pit is a UNESCO World Heritage Centre in Darmstadt-Dieburg, Germany. It is a small site about 1 km long and 700 m wide and is the source of the best-preserved fossils in the world that represent the Eocene Age, i.e. from 57 to 36 million years ago. Their remarkable preservation is due to their position in deep layers of protective sediment. The Eocene is of particular interest as it was a time of significant mammal development.

would have been twenty years ago. It's hard to work out of the public gaze these days and there are some good things about that. But, we do still have to apply proper scientific method before we make statements to the wider world."

"Yeah," grunted Alec. "Look, I need to get back to the labs. Would you make my apologies or goodbyes to whoever needs to be stroked?"

Alec put down his drink and walked quickly to the exit, head down. Joseph watched him go, shaking his head slightly, as Juliet made her way over to him.

"Has Alec gone already?" she asked.

"Yes, he's eager to get back to the lab. It's understandable, Juliet. He said thanks for the reception, though."

She looked at him sceptically. "I'll bet he did. Did you manage to have a word with him about our conversation earlier?"

"Yes, I did, and he seems to understand. Didn't make his day though."

"No, I'm sure. Well, let's hope that we can have a period of peace and quiet now while he gets on with his analysis."

"We can but hope," sighed Joseph.

His hopes were not to be realised.

5

Over the five weeks leading up to the Easter break Alec and his students worked long hours, gently cleaning the remains and shellfish, and gradually laying them out to investigate the morphology. Alec worked very late most evenings on his own and the university security staff began to get used to him being there on their evening rounds. Usually the swipe card access was disabled at night and the doors locked, but special arrangements had been made for this project and so swipe access was available twenty-four hours a day. Alec often worked on until ten pm, occasionally even later, long after his colleagues had given up for the evening and gone to live their lives outside the lab.

But Alec didn't really have a life outside the lab. He didn't have much of a life outside his own head. That had always been one of the reasons his many romantic relationships had ended. There had been no shortage of candidates, although the women who were interested in Alec generally had to work fairly hard to get noticed. He was a physically fit and good-looking man and he found women sexually attractive, but he could not seem to recognise the social cues that might show him that a woman was interested in him. And then, sooner or later, his relationships ended because he was never able to connect across the emotional gap. No matter how good the sex was.

Fortunately for him, technology had come to the rescue as far as some other forms of human interaction were concerned. He had really taken to social networking technologies. Communication without immediate personal contact was perfect for him. And the type of communication suited him, too. He could write as much or as little as he liked about exactly what absorbed him. He didn't have to bother whether other people were interested, bored, or any other of the many human emotions that he had always found it so difficult to pick up on. He didn't have to answer questions if he didn't want to; didn't have to look anyone in the face and try to read what they were feeling. He had never been able to do that successfully in any case. Joseph was very good at it, he realised that, but to Alec it was an occult art. So he blogged and Tweeted and took little notice of any comments or responses to his postings. Until the last couple of weeks, when he had spotted three or four comments on his blog that had been a little ... different. Not directly threatening, but written in a strange style. He thought it was probably just somebody having a go at him so he didn't approve them, but he did decide that he would show them to Joseph soon. Just to see what he thought about them.

The room was shadowy and cold. April evening sunlight was fading to scarlet as the balding man lit the candle and placed it on the dark mahogany dresser by the wall. The flickering flame illuminated a picture directly above it; a monk, tonsured and in a medieval habit. The candlelight reflected off a cut-throat razor lying with its blade open on the dresser top, directly underneath the picture. He picked up the razor and laid the cold metal flat against the skin on the uppermost surface of his left arm.

"This is your day, William. It is only fitting that I make this dedication." He pulled the razor across his arm, shaving away the hair in a crescent swathe. "When we shave away all superfluous explanations, what remains is the truth." He tilted the back of the razor up, the sharp edge pressing an indentation into his skin, then pulled the blade slowly towards his body. "But sometimes the truth must hurt."

Blood oozed out of the deep cut and trickled along his arm in a dark red rivulet, two small drops falling onto the parquet floor before he could staunch the flow with tissues. The monk in the picture looked on impassively as the man hurried from the room and climbed the stairs to the bathroom. There he took a pack of plasters out of a cabinet on the wall and peeled the backing strip away from a large one. Pulling the tissues off the cut he quickly applied the plaster, washed his hands and then dried them on the grimy towel hanging on the back of the bathroom door. He went back downstairs, pulled on his raincoat and returned to the candlelit room. He looked up at the picture with reverence. "I trust you will approve of my offering," he whispered, picking up the blooded razor and pulling the hood of his coat up over his head. He blew out the candle and hurried out of the house.

6

Whistling to himself, Joseph swiped his access card to open the lab door. *Seven thirty in the morning,* he thought, *I must be keen.* Alec had called him the previous evening, almost breathless with excitement. He had just finished the cleaning and reconstruction of the skull, and his research team had freed all the other bones from the surrounding matrix. Alec had told Joseph very little, except that her cranial capacity was around eight-hundred and fifty cubic centimetres, her fingers were long and curved and that the reconstruction of her pelvis made it clear that she had been bipedal in life. The shape of her skull made her look like an early *Homo ergaster*, but this was all pretty much what everyone had expected and didn't explain why Alec was so excited. He wouldn't tell Joseph anything on the phone, though. He said he had something that Joseph just had to see.

On entering the lab he quickly became aware of a strange smell. He was used to the dusty, earthy smell of remains and dry bones, but this was different. More metallic. More organic. As he walked further into the lab he saw that two trolleys had been placed side by side. On one were the fossilised bones, laid out in the recognisable shape of a humanoid skeleton. The skull had been reconstructed and lay, face up, with six of the fossilised shellfish placed around it. On the neighbouring trolley was Alec, naked, laid out on his back with six fresh mussels placed around his head. Blood that had flowed from a wound to the back of his head, low down near the base of his skull, lay in a dark, congealed pool on the trolley. His eyes were wide open, staring unseeingly at the ceiling. Joseph's first urge was to run; his second was to be sick. He followed both urges in rapid succession. When he emerged from the lab toilet he stood in the outer office, trying to regain control of himself until he was able to think more clearly. When he had stopped shaking quite so violently he picked up the phone to call Security.

"This is Doctor Connor in Lab G0 twelve. I think there's been some kind of accident here. Doctor Whickham's been ... Could someone get down here quickly?"

"Should I call for a first-aider too?" came the reply.

Joseph could feel a hysterical laugh forcing its way up from his chest. He swallowed it down hard. "No, I don't think that will be necessary. I think you should call the police and an ambulance though. Yes, the police, right now. I think Doctor Whickham is dead."

They sat in the empty classroom. The strengthening spring sunshine filtered through the grime on the windows, casting geometric patterns on the wall and floor. No one would remember this as a sunny day, though. Detective Inspector Elaine Kelly smiled at Joseph across the table. Her long, dark hair was held back with a large metal comb that flashed reflected sunlight as she bent her head to see over the top of her reading glasses. Detective Sergeant Jack Robson sat to her left, taking notes of the interview, and a portable recorder sat on the table between them. Kelly spoke to it.

"Eleventh of April at thirteen forty-five. Interviewing Doctor Joseph Connor." She turned to Joseph. "I'm sorry you've had to wait around in the university all morning, Doctor Connor. It's taken some time for the SOCO team and the pathologist to do their stuff. And we've been waiting for some information requests to come back. Perhaps we could start by you telling me what happened in your own words, please?"

Joseph nodded. "Yes, sure. Well, Alec called me yesterday to ask me to meet him at the labs first thing this morning. He'd just finished the preliminary cleaning and restructuring of the finds and he wanted me to take a look."

"Why you?"

"Oh, well, I was Alec's PhD supervisor at Birmingham ten years ago. We've worked together quite a bit since then. I suppose I'm what passed for one of Alec's closest friends. He didn't have many." Joseph paused.

"Go on," said Kelly.

"So, I came down to the labs at about half seven this morning, let myself in and then found Alec as you saw him."

"Did you touch anything?" asked Kelly.

"No."

"And then you called Security?"

"No," admitted Joseph. "I went to be sick. Then I called Security."

"Did you go back into the lab after your call?"

"No, I didn't. Lily, Egraine and Ben arrived and so I was occupied with telling them what had happened. They didn't go into the lab, though. None of us were feeling too well so we just waited for the police. Oh, the security manager came down with some tea, but he didn't go into the lab."

"Your ID card gives you access to the labs twenty-four hours a day, does it?" asked Kelly.

"Yes."

"I have to ask you this, Doctor Connor. Where were you at around nine thirty last night?"

"At home."

"Can anyone vouch for that?" asked Kelly

"Yes, my wife, my daughter and her friend who was round for dinner."

"Did you leave the house at any time?"

"No, I didn't."

"Thank you, I'm sure you'll appreciate that we have to ask everyone with access to the labs the same question."

"Of course," said Joseph, trying to hide the fact that he was beginning to shake. He'd seen this kind of thing on TV, but to be actually asked to account for himself was devastating in a way he would never have believed.

"Good. Just a few last questions about Doctor Whickham, if you're still feeling OK?"

"Yes, I'm OK. Just rather shaky."

"I'd have thought you'd be used to dead bodies," said Robson. "Don't you dig them up for a living?" Kelly shot Robson a disapproving look.

Joseph bristled. "Well, not really. I'm a paleobiologist, not an archaeologist. In any case, the dead bodies I work with on occasions aren't friends of mine and they've been dead for long enough to begin to fossilise. Rather different."

Kelly nodded. "Of course, but it would be helpful for me to know a little about Doctor

Whickham. Was he popular? You seemed to imply before that he didn't have many friends."

"Alec was an introverted man," replied Joseph, trying to think of the best way to describe his dead friend. "Practical and unemotional, I would say. A good man at heart and very intelligent, but not very good with people." *I wonder if understatement is an offence*, he thought to himself.

"Had he fallen out with anyone in particular just recently?"

"Not really," said Joseph. "Not especially. I suppose."

"You seem hesitant, Doctor Connor. I need to press you to give me straight answers."

"Well, Alec upset a lot of people. That's how he was. But nothing very out of the ordinary just lately," he lied. *OK, so Alec and Juliet had fallen out badly over this find, but not to the point of murder. That was ridiculous.*

"How was his relationship with Professor Bailey?" Kelly's head tilted slightly as she asked the question.

Joseph flinched. *That's weird; can she read my mind?* "Erm, well, they didn't see eye to eye on a lot of things, but just academic cut and thrust, you know. Why?"

Kelly's demeanour suddenly hardened. "Because Professor Bailey's ID card was used to access room G0 twelve at nine twenty-five last night. No one can verify her whereabouts at the time and she's currently accompanying one of my officers to the station. That's why. So if you know anything about their relationship, Doctor Connor, you'd better tell me now."

7

Juliet sat in the interview room, staring absently at the red light on the recording machine as it burned a steady red.

"Professor Bailey?" No response. "Professor Bailey?" Kelly was louder this time.

Juliet looked startled. "Yes, sorry."

"Do you wish to have a legal representative with you?"

Juliet shook her head.

"OK, for the record the time is five thirty-five pm on the eleventh of April. DI Kelly and DS Robson interviewing Professor Juliet Bailey. Professor Bailey has declined legal representation at this time."

Juliet sat with her right leg wrapped around her left, her arms folded tight against her chest. She looked like a coiled spring and seemed to be concentrating very hard on the top of the table in front of her.

Kelly recited the obligatory caution and then asked, "Professor Bailey, could you give us an account of your movements yesterday evening please?"

"I left the university around six thirty and went straight home. I was there for the remainder of the evening," Juliet replied, keeping her eyes firmly fixed on one of the coffee mug rings on the grimy table top.

"Can anyone vouch for your movements after you left the university?"

"No, I live alone. I was working on a paper. I had some supper when I got in at about seven and then worked on the paper until gone eleven. Then I went to bed."

"If that is the case, can you explain how your ID card was used to open the laboratory door at nine twenty-five pm yesterday?" asked Kelly

"No, I can't," replied Juliet wretchedly. "I have no idea how that could have happened."

"Did you have your ID card with you last night?" asked Kelly

"Yes, I did." Still no eye contact.

"Did you kill Alec Whickham?" asked Robson, straight to the point.

"No, of course not. I would never kill anyone." Juliet began to shake as tears welled in her eyes.

"We understand that you've been having a disagreement with Doctor Whickham over his work." Kelly again. "Quite a strong disagreement, according to some witnesses who heard your argument yesterday morning. You were pretty agitated, by all accounts. What was that disagreement about?"

Juliet looked up suddenly and began to become excited, seeming to lose some of her earlier meekness. "Alec had been making claims about what his find proves in relation to human evolution and the role played by water. I feel very strongly that those claims are premature, and could leave the university in a vulnerable position regarding future research funding. I had repeatedly asked Alec to be more measured and to tone down his claims. I don't believe he really understood the wider picture."

"And did his work threaten your reputation?" asked Robson

"Of course not! That's an outrageous accusation! My work has a solid, evidential base of more than twenty years research. What are you suggesting? That I killed Alec because I thought he might be right and I might be wrong? I'm a career academic, for God's sake! If academics went around killing colleagues who disagreed with them or challenged their work the universities in this country would be depopulated in a matter of months." Juliet's face was very red as she leaned forward across the table.

Better step in here. I've got a more soothing voice than Jack. Hell, everyone has a more soothing voice than Jack thought Kelly to herself. "Please try to stay calm, Professor Bailey. Let's go back to yesterday evening. Did you call anyone, or did anyone call you? Anyone at all who could corroborate your claim to be at home all evening?"

Juliet took a deep breath and sat back. "No, I always put my answerphone on when I'm working, and don't usually have my mobile switched on as a matter of course. I like to be left alone to work."

"What did you have for supper?"

Juliet paused, surprised at the sudden change of tack. "Er, salad, a little cheese and some bread, I think."

"Have you prepared any meat at home over the past couple of days?

Juliet's brow wrinkled. "No. I'm a vegetarian. What a strange question."

"Have you cut yourself at all over the past couple of days?"

"What? No!"

"So, how do you explain the blood-stained absorbent paper that my SOCO team have just found in your dustbin?"

Juliet uncrossed her legs and sat up straight, suddenly regaining her customary composure. "I've changed my mind. I do not wish to answer any further questions until I have legal representation."

8

The following morning Joseph and Mike were the only two customers in the Java Man [3]coffee bar, just down the corridor from their office. They sat by the window, looking out at the trees being bent by a blustery breeze. The university was eerily quiet over the Easter break; most of the undergraduates had gone home for the holidays and only some overseas students and the keener postgraduates were still around.

"I simply do not believe it," said Joseph. "It just doesn't add up. They didn't like each other but she's got no motive to kill him. And anyway, Alec was a strong guy; surely she doesn't have the strength to hit him hard enough to kill him? And she's nowhere near strong enough to heave him onto a trolley. And anyway, this is Juliet we're talking about!"

---

[3] Java Man is the name given to remains discovered in 1891 on the banks of the Solo River in East Java, Indonesia. It was one of the first known specimens of *Homo erectus*. Until older human remains were discovered in the Great Rift Valley in Kenya, these discoveries were the oldest hominin remains ever found. It was therefore suggested at the time that Java Man was an intermediate hominin between modern humans and the human/chimp common ancestor, but the current anthropological and genetic consensus is that the direct ancestors of modern humans were African populations of *Homo erectus* or *Homo ergaster* (the names are somewhat interchangeable), rather than the Asian populations of which Java Man is an example. Note that Java Man was discovered by a river, though.

"But, to play devil's advocate for a minute," replied Mike, half wincing as he knew this would be unpopular with Joseph, "she was very upset with him a couple of days ago, shouting at him in the corridor. I've never seen her do that before. And it isn't so much how hard you hit someone as where, for it to be most effective. By going in low at the base of the skull the spinal cord is severed where it enters the cranial cavity. And Juliet has an excellent understanding of human anatomy. And she's over an inch taller than Alec, I'd say. And lastly, the trolleys wind down so she wouldn't have to lift him up to waist height, just roll him onto the trolley at ground level. Sorry, for all those 'counter-ands', but for the sake of balance you should consider them."

Joseph stared into his coffee. "OK, so it is physically possible, but I still can't credit that Juliet would do such a thing. And leave a trail a mile wide behind her."

"Mm," agreed Mike. "Actually that is one of the things that makes it seem unlikely to me. She's smarter than that. Although I guess the police are thinking crime of passion, spur of the moment stuff. There are questions to answer though, so I guess that's why she's been kept in overnight."

Joseph's mobile rang at that moment. "Oh, Inspector Kelly. Hello." Pause. "Yes, sure, I can be down there in about fifteen minutes. Bye"

Mike raised his eyebrows. "The police want to see you again?"

"Apparently."

"Be careful Joseph. That loyalty of yours can be a positive attribute, but it is possible for it to be misplaced sometimes. Just don't get yourself involved in this any further."

Joseph smiled at his colleague. "Don't worry, I won't," he lied. *I seem to be lying more than usual these days.*

Kelly sat down on the other side of the table in the interview room.

"Thanks for coming, Doctor Connor. It's just to clear up one or two things that have come to light during our questioning of Professor Bailey."

"Sure."

"Yesterday Professor Bailey claimed to have remembered that she lost her ID card for a brief period a few weeks ago. She says that she had to phone you on her mobile from the front door of the building so you could come down to let her in one morning. Her PA wasn't answering her phone, apparently, and yours was the only other extension number she had listed on her mobile. Do you remember this?"

Joseph thought for a moment. "Actually, yes, I do."

"Could you describe to me what happened?"

"Yes, it'd be about two weeks ago. I got a call from Juliet just after I'd come into the office one morning, so it'd be around eight thirty. She said she'd got to the door that morning and couldn't find her ID card in her bag. She seemed a bit puzzled as she was sure that she'd put it back in there the previous day. I let her in and then we checked her office, but we couldn't find it."

"Did it turn up?"

"Yes, it did. Later that day she told me that she'd found the card under some of the papers on her desk. She thought she must have left it there the previous day and forgotten that she hadn't put it in her bag. That was it really. She didn't seem to think anything else of it."

"Do you think it was taken or that Professor Bailey mislaid it?"

"I don't know. Could be either, I suppose. My guess was that she'd probably left it on her desk when she thought she'd put it back in her bag. Easily done."

A young officer put her head around the interview room door. "Excuse me Ma'am, the CCTV footage is ready."

"OK, thanks Sharon. Well, thanks for coming in Doctor Connor. If anything else comes up I may need to speak to you again." Kelly stood up. Joseph didn't.

"There's just one thing I wanted to mention to you. It struck me after our interview yesterday."

"Go on," said Kelly, sitting down again.

"Well, it may be nothing, but Alec did tell me a couple of weeks ago that he'd been getting strange comments left on his blog. Not the sort of stuff he usually got, but a bit, well, odd. A sort of warning about his work."

"What sort of thing?"

"Well, creationist and biblical references."

"Are you a good friend of Professor Bailey, Doctor Connor?" asked Kelly, with a slightly weary expression.

"A friend and colleague. I've known Juliet for ten years. Since I first started at UNWE."

"I know it can be hard to accept sometimes that we don't know people as well as we think we do," said Kelly, pushing her chair back with a grinding squeak that set Joseph's teeth on edge. "But I come across all kinds of people in this job. I can just about believe anything about anybody. Excuse me, I must go."

She opened the door for Joseph and ushered him out to the front desk. "Thanks again, Doctor Connor."

Kelly went back along the corridor to another room and sat down next to Robson. "What does the CCTV tell us then?" she asked.

"Not a lot really," he replied. "The only coverage is outside the front of the science building and the lighting isn't too good. Take a look."

He pressed the remote button to play the first video clip. The screen flickered into life, showing a fuzzy image of the front of the science building and the date and time stamp of tenth of April at twenty-one twenty-five. A figure appeared, walking across to the front of the building and carrying a small bag. Dressed in dark trousers and a raincoat with the hood up, the figure walked to the front door, swiped an ID card and then entered. He or she was about five feet eight inches tall, medium build. The second clip was time stamped twenty-two sixteen and showed what looked like the same person walking out of the front door, head down and carrying the same bag.

"Could be anyone," said Robson. "Doesn't prove it's her, but it certainly doesn't rule her out either. What did Doctor Connor have to say about her missing ID card story?"

"Well, it checks out with him. Although I rather think our Doctor Connor is very keen to support her however he can. Would you talk to her PA and see if she heard anything about it?"

"Yeah, sure" said Robson, getting up to leave.

Kelly leaned back in the chair. "You know, I'd be happier if we could find the weapon. It can't be that easy to dispose of something covered in that much blood. And why would she be daft enough to put the blood stained paper in her own bin? She's a professor, for Christ's sake!"

Robson turned around. "True. But, it's still looking like there's too much evidence against her."

"Yes, there is," said Kelly thoughtfully. "Far too much."

9

Joseph walked back into his office to see Mike standing at the window again. He turned around. "What was all that about?"

"Juliet told them about mislaying her ID card a few weeks ago and they just wanted me to corroborate it."

"And did you?"

"Yes, of course. It happened exactly as they said Juliet had described it," replied Joseph, walking over to the kettle and clicking it on.

"Yeah, actually, I remember that too," said Mike. "But what's that got to do with her card being used yesterday? She didn't claim to have lost it again did she?"

"No. I don't really know why they thought it was significant. Just checking what Juliet had told them, I guess."

"So, it's still looking grim for her, is it?" asked Mike.

"Yes, I think it is. I did tell them about those weird blog postings Alec had been getting though."

"What weird blog postings?"

"Oh, didn't he tell you? Someone has been writing creationist and biblical stuff in the comments section of his blog, apparently. He didn't authorise them so they never showed up publicly, but he did keep copies of them, so he said."

"What kinds of things had they been writing?" asked Mike.

"Well, a bit out of the ordinary. At first he didn't worry about them, but he said the last one sounded threatening."

"And what did the police think when you told them?" asked Mike.

"Kelly didn't take it seriously at all," replied Joseph.

"Well maybe you ought to give them to Kelly so she can see for herself."

"Alec didn't give me a copy of them. They'll be on his computer so we can't get at them."

"Wanna bet?" asked Mike, with a twinkle.

"Whoa, hacking into someone else's computer is a serious thing to do Mike." He paused for a moment. "Anyway, how would you do it? The place is crawling with police, the labs and Alec's office are cordoned off and I wouldn't be surprised if they've taken his computer away."

"We don't need his computer," said Mike. "All we need is access to his network drives. I bet we can guess Alec's password if we try hard enough. We know his username, that's no secret."

"I guess it would be helping Juliet out," Joseph rationalised.

"I just hope he didn't save the document to his local drive," said Mike. "If he did, we're stuffed. I guess the police may have got the IT department to restrict access to his network drives too. So it's a long shot anyway." He looked at Joseph with an almost adolescent grin. "Let's do it!"

Mike sat down in front of his computer and logged off from his account. "OK, we'll try logging in as Alec. We know that Alec's username was ar-whickham. No secret there." Mike typed it into the username box. "So, here we start guessing passwords. Any ideas?"

"Well," said Joseph, "no. Oh, what about aquatic ape allusions. Try 'aquaticape'."

Mike tried it and hit return. "Nope, invalid password. What else?"

"We could try mixes of 'aquatic', 'ape', 'water' and 'hypothesis' I guess," Joseph suggested.

They tried two or three combinations of words, but all came back as invalid.

"We're going to get locked out of trying here soon. Come on Joe, let's have one of your blinding flashes of inspiration!"

Joseph thought. *What really mattered to Alec? What would always be important, defining, to him?*

"Try 'scarsofevolution'."

"What?"

Joseph spelled it out for him. Mike hit the return key and the screen showed the university generic background and login dialogue box.

"Yes! It'll take a minute or two to get in. Then we need to find the document with the blog postings."

"You know we could get fired for this, don't you? The university has very strict rules about security and identity."

"Look," replied Mike, "we just print out a copy of the document here and then you say that Alec gave you a copy of the blog postings. Simple. This could be really important for Juliet."

"Yes, I know. OK, what have we got then?"

"Let's have a look at his files. Alec was one tidy man, that's for sure. Ah, there's a folder called blog. Sounds like a good starting point." Mike opened the folder and a list of documents appeared.

"There's one here called 'creationist postings".
Let's try that."

The Word document opened and Mike and
Joseph read the text.

February 28th 14:30

1. You leave a significant gap in
possible explanations for this poor creature's
death. The Bible tells us of the Flood, of water
coming from the earth and from the sky.
Recent scientific enquiry has shown that there
is enough water in the earth's mantle to fill
the seas many times over, and rain could fall
from the sky for 40 days and 40 nights for a
number of reasons, such as:

• Collapse of a thick water-vapour
canopy which surrounded the pre-Flood
earth high in the atmosphere. Calculations
indicate this could not have held much water,
but it may explain some.

• Jets of water shooting high into the
atmosphere from under the earth and falling
back as rain.

• Intense cyclones called hypercanes
that developed over warm ocean water
(heated by underwater volcanic eruptions).

• Water dumped on the earth by a
swarm of comets. The craters on the moon
point to an intense solar system
bombardment, and some creationists suggest
this happened during the Flood.

• A combination of these.

As you are a scientist and an academic, I give you the reference for the above extract: Walker T, 2008. Creation, 30:2, 55.

March 4th 10:48

2. I wait for your reply, Doctor Whickham, but none comes. How do you answer the main problem with the fossil record? That it shows no examples of one species turning into another. No one would argue that there is no diversity within species. Clearly we can see different breeds of dogs, cats, and Darwin's favourite, pigeons. But these are "of a kind". What makes you think that your fossil specimen is not of a kind with other apes?

March 9th 09:07

3. Are you ever going to debate this with me? My motives for saying these things are partly to help you to protect your immortal soul. The intention is the same as the deed. God who knows the heart, accepteth the affect for the effect, and the will for the deed.

March 15th 08:11

4. Remember what the Bible tells us. That Balaam desired to die the death of the righteous, but that was impossible, because he lived not the life of the righteous. None can learn the art of dying well, without the life of righteousness. Augustus Caesar wished a good death, but he knew not what it meant:

only the righteous are capable of it. If you were to die soon, your soul would not be ready, Doctor Whickham.

"Christ," whispered Mike. "This turns into really odd stuff at the end. Did Alec tell you they were like this?"

"No, he didn't say exactly what had been written, but it did concern him. Reading it now I'm not surprised."

"The police have got to see this. Fortunately Alec made notes of the dates and times of the postings so the blog provider could check for accesses to the blog at those times and get the IP addresses of the computers, I guess."

"Get the what?" asked Joseph.

"IP addresses. Unique numbers that identify computers on the web. It might tell us which computers were used to access the blog. Doesn't necessarily tell you who was using them of course, but it might be a start."

"Let's just print this off and get out of Alec's files," said Joseph, as Mike closed the folder and went back to Windows Explorer. Then Joseph spotted a folder with the title 'Watermark paper - drafts'. "Oh, hey, just before we do, can you open that Watermark folder?"

Mike double-clicked on the icon. The folder contained several documents, but Joseph's eye was drawn to 'Watermark latest draft'.

"Can you print that off for me as well?" asked Joseph.

"Getting a feel for this eh?" joked Mike, and then he saw Joseph's face. "Oh, hey, sorry, I know he'd been your student and was still your friend. This must be hard for you."

"This is a new paper, I'm sure," said Joseph. "I'd like to see Alec's last work. He had tremendous talent, you know, for all his social difficulties."

Mike nodded, sent the document to the printer and then logged off from Alec's account.

"Can't help feeling a bit naughty, but righteous too," said Mike.

Joseph nodded. "But now it raises the question of what to do next. Should I call the police and give them the blog postings, or wait?"

"You said that they didn't seem interested, so I think you'll wait a long time."

"Well, I've had quite enough excitement for one week. We're going to the cottage this weekend for a break, so I think I'll have more stomach for this on Monday. I'll call the police then. There's nothing more we can do for now."

Joseph and Anna owned a cottage on the Lancashire coast at Lytham St Anne's. Anna's father had left it to her when he died and as an only child she didn't have to worry about selling it to split the inheritance, so they had kept it as a weekend retreat. When the kids were younger they had loved their weekends by the seaside, but now it was more often just Joseph and Anna who stayed there to recharge their batteries. This particular weekend was a mild and sunny lull in the otherwise blustery, showery spring weather. The kind of day that gives just a hint that summer is not too far away.

It was Sunday morning and they had gone down to one of their favourite haunts on this underrated coastline, to stroll along the beach at Formby. They hadn't yet managed to spot one of the rare red squirrels that lived in the woodland that backed onto the sand dunes, but they lived in hope. Socks and shoes off, they waded for an hour along the shoreline. The beach was speckled with residents and visitors, making the most of the mild sunshine that sparkled across the water.

"Whatever the rights and wrongs of human evolution theories, we sure do love the water," said Joseph, watching children playing dare with the small waves and collecting water in buckets to fill their sandcastle moats. It was low tide and in the mud flats they could see a gazebo covering one of the archaeological sites that only becomes visible for a short time every day. Footprints that are around five thousand years old appear here, capturing points in time when human hunter-gatherers walked through the sand and mud; fishing, scavenging and hunting deer and giant aurochs, which also left their hoof prints in the Mesolithic mud. The environment then was rather different; marshier, with lagoons and rivers running down towards a more distant shoreline. Most Mesolithic peoples lived predominantly near rivers, coasts and waterways, echoing the routes of their ancestors when they left Africa some seventy thousand years earlier.

"Well, the seaside always make me hungry," said Anna. "And I really fancy fish and chips."

"What a surprise! Don't tell me – the Crispy Cod in Formby."

Anna chuckled as they pulled their socks and shoes back on, ignoring the wet sand between their toes. "Race you back to the car. Last one there's driving!" She sprinted off, her shoulder-length blonde hair bobbing in the breeze, while Joseph hopped after her, trying to get his remaining shoe back on.

"Hey, not fair! No warning!" He started to chase her, unknowingly following a line of ancient footprints captured in the mud beneath the fine, golden sand.

A half-empty red wine bottle stood on the coffee table. Anna snoozed on the sofa with her feet across Joseph's lap, whilst he read Alec's paper. Fifteen minutes later he put the paper down on the table, yawned and stretched. Anna stirred. "How was it?" she asked sleepily.

"Very interesting."

"What's wrong? You've got that look you get when you're not sure about something." She swung her legs off his lap and sat up.

"It's a pretty big departure from fundamental AAH. And it doesn't read like Alec's style really. It looks to me like he was collaborating with someone. But there's no other attribution." He paused for a moment. "What does a capital A followed by a question mark mean to you?"

"Nothing."

"Me neither." He shook his head. "Either someone finally got through to him about weighing evidence, or this paper was at least partly written by someone else."

"Who?" she asked, standing up and pulling him off the sofa.

He stretched again. "Good question."

She took his hand and led him towards the stairs. "Well, it's one for tomorrow. Time for bed."

10

Joseph came into the office on Monday morning just as his telephone began to ring. He picked it up.

"Hello, Joseph Connor."

"Hi, Doctor Connor." It was Kelly's voice. "I was wondering if you would be around this morning. If I could come over to see you?"

"Yes, of course. Is it about anything in particular?"

"Something you said on Friday that perhaps I dismissed too quickly. About threatening emails or something?" Kelly's voice sounded less sure today than previously; softer somehow.

"Oh, the blog postings. Yes, well, coincidentally I was going to call you today to have another go at getting you to listen to me. I've got a copy of them and I really do think you should see them."

"I'll be over at about eleven thirty, if that suits you?" Her voice softened further. "I have to attend Doctor Whickham's post mortem in about ten minutes."

He swallowed. "Oh, yes, of course. I'll see you here then? Or shall we meet somewhere?"

"I'll be ready for a strong coffee I think. PMs aren't my favourite part of the job, I'm afraid. I'll see you in the coffee shop just down the road from your building?"

"That's fine," he replied, "I'll be there at eleven thirty."

"I may be a little delayed, but I'll call you on your mobile if it looks like I won't make it. If something comes up at the PM."

"Sure, of course. See you later."

Joseph put the phone down and sat behind his desk, but immediately got up again and walked over to the window. He just couldn't concentrate on anything other than Alec's death at the moment. The sadness and shock were paralysing, but they were also tinged with curiosity. Who could possibly have wanted to do this to Alec, and have the capability to do it too? Also, as the initial shock had worn off, many people in the university were beginning to feel vulnerable and threatened. What if this was some madman who would strike again? Was it a one off, just Alec, or did they have a maniac on the loose in the university?

He worked fitfully until eleven fifteen, mainly thinking through the draft of Alec's paper he had read the previous evening. Then, taking the blog postings and a copy of Alec's paper with him, he left his office and walked down the street to the coffee bar at the bottom of the hill. Kelly wasn't there when he arrived, so he got himself a large latte and sat in an easy chair by the window.

Alec's paper fascinated him. But it also concerned him for a reason he couldn't quite pin down. Although it read like his writing in places, and Joseph had plenty of experience of reading Alec's work, the content was more of a mixture. Either he had suddenly developed the ability to read and assimilate more widely, or someone else had been involved in this paper. *But who? And why would Alec not recognise that contribution in the author attribution?*

Joseph was roused from these thoughts by Kelly's arrival.

"Hi," he said. "Can I get you something?"

She sat down heavily, looking pale and drawn. "I'll have a double shot espresso please."

Joseph went over to order and came and sat down again whilst the barista ground the coffee.

"Was it rough?" he asked.

She nodded and sighed deeply. "Brains. I'm not too bad with most bits of the human body, but brains really get to me. It would be a head injury, wouldn't it?"

"No doubt that's what killed him, then?"

"Well, it's looking most likely. The toxicology reports will take a few days, but cause of death appears to be a blow to the back of his head, just at the base of the skull, with a pointed object. Well, more like a pointed wedge, apparently. Like a very wide, thick arrow head. The pathologist was a bit stumped as to what could make that kind of wound."

Joseph went cold. "Might be a hand axe."

"A what?"

"A stone hand axe. Nimue probably died around one and a half million years ago. At that time human ancestors were beginning to make tools in what's called the Acheulean Tradition. It's also known as the great hand axe tradition. I could draw one for you if you have something I could draw on. "

"Nimue," said Kelly. "Very apt. The lady of the lake".

Joseph smiled as a call of "double espresso!!" came from the barista.

Kelly went to retrieve her coffee and came back with a handful of napkins. "I left my notebook in the office. How about drawing on one of these?" She put them down on the table between them.

Joseph took out his pen and drew a large tear drop shape with a pointed end, swearing under his breath as the fragile paper tore a little. "OK, so, they're generally this sort of shape. They're usually heavily worked so they have a large number of percussive facets all over them, like this. But, I have to say, I'm a biologist and no expert in tool traditions."

"Who is?" asked Kelly, sipping her coffee and grimacing slightly as the dark, bitter liquid hit her tongue. Joseph looked at the floor.

"Ah," she said. "Professor Bailey?"

He nodded. "But I'm sure she doesn't carry them around in her handbag, just in case she feels like murdering someone!"

"No, but she has stone tools in the display case in her office, doesn't she? Does she have a hand axe?"

Joseph nodded again. "Perhaps someone broke in and took it to kill Alec."

"Or perhaps the spectre of his dead specimen rose up and killed him with a ghostly hand axe!" said Kelly sarcastically, but Joseph didn't laugh. She leaned forward and her face softened a little. "There was no sign of her office being broken into on the night Doctor Whickham was killed. Sorry, I know you're Professor Bailey's friend and colleague, but I have to follow the evidence. My job is to stay as impartial as possible. As a scientist, I'm sure you understand the principle of objective investigation."

Joseph looked at her quizzically. "Spoken like a scientist."

She leaned back in her chair. "A first degree in chemistry and a Masters in forensics. Your next question is why am I a copper then?" He nodded as she sipped more of her coffee. "I like solving puzzles, I guess."

"Well, here's another one." He smiled, putting a paper down on the table between them. "These are the blog postings I was talking about."

She read them with growing disquiet. "Hmm. I see. Well, Doctor Whickham must have been concerned to keep a copy, and to give you one."

Joseph blushed and looked sheepish. Kelly saw it. "Where did you get this document from?" she asked.

"From his network drive on Friday. Sorry, I really thought it might be important. It's a disciplinary offence to do that, so if you could keep that particular bit of information under your hat I'd be grateful."

She gave him a disapproving look. "If you promise not to play detective again, Doctor Connor."

He nodded.

Retrieving her mobile phone from her bag, she made a speed dial call. "Hi Jack. Listen, these blog postings do turn rather threatening. Could you take a look at Doctor Whickham's blog and see which provider he was with, and then contact them and ask if they have IP address records for these accesses? You ready?" She read out the four dates and their corresponding times. "Thanks. Call me as soon as you get anything. Yep, I am. Bye."

She turned back to Joseph. "OK, so, let's suppose for a moment that all the evidence against Professor Bailey has been planted, someone else killed Doctor Whickham and they're attempting to frame the good professor. This is just hypothetical, you understand. Purely a mind exercise that you might help me with. You know how the university works and I don't."

"Now you're talking!" said Joseph with enthusiasm. "Hypothetically, of course."

Kelly leaned over the table. "So, I'm an old-fashioned girl. Means, motive and opportunity. Let's think about means first."

"Well," said Joseph, "I guess the first stumbling block is Juliet's card being used to enter the labs at the time Alec was killed. There were no other accesses at that time?"

"No, the security guards had done their previous round at eight thirty and weren't due back until midnight," Kelly confirmed.

"So how do we get past that one?"

"Well, actually," she replied, "it is possible to clone the type of swipe card that you use at the university. It would be similar to the way stolen credit card details are cloned onto fake cards. The professor did lose sight of her card for the best part of twenty-four hours a few weeks ago, as you confirmed."

"Christ! Cloned? Well, that makes the missing card really compelling evidence, doesn't it?"

"Not necessarily. It would be easy for Professor Bailey to claim that her card had gone missing and set up the whole stunt of asking you to let her in. Although, that makes the whole thing look more premeditated, and the rest of the evidence against her points more to something done on the spur of the moment and poorly covered up. Except the mussels around Whickham's head. That looks premeditated too. That's why I'm struggling a bit with this whole thing. It doesn't smell right. Hmm, perhaps you should ignore that last sentence."

"Why?"

"Because the weight of evidence against the professor is very strong. I can't go on hunches and feelings. I have to find good, solid, empirical facts."

"So," said Joseph thoughtfully, "we might be looking for someone who was able to steal Juliet's ID card from her bag without her knowledge."

"How likely do you think that is, knowing the professor's habits and the general level of security in the faculty?" asked Kelly.

"Well she does leave her office door open on occasions, sometimes when she's nipped out to chat in the faculty."

"So it would be possible for someone to dash in, steal the card and dash out again. Or, steal the card when in her office for a meeting if she were called out for some reason. Who does that narrow it down to?"

Joseph smiled. "Well, the first scenario narrows it down to more than a hundred academic, professional and support staff, a couple of thousand students and anyone any of those people brought in with them. Rather a large potential field. If you're thinking about it being taken by someone she was meeting in her office, I guess her diary will show who came to see her that day, but only if it was a previous appointment. But anyway, surely it's just too risky. The thief could so easily get caught."

"True, but it's only a minute of a job if they know where to look. Even if they didn't know, they could take an educated guess and look in her bag. If it's not there then they watch her and try again another day." Kelly pondered. "Then once they've got the card, they need access to cloning systems. Or to other people who can do it for them. You have a computing department at the university?"

"We do, but not on this site. The Technology Faculty is on another part of the campus across town." Joseph scratched his head. "You keep saying 'they'. Is that to avoid the gender trap or do you think there was more than one of them?"

"A bit of both. If what we're discussing did happen, or something like it, it would take some planning. Maybe one person could do it, I don't know. I can't get a clear enough picture yet. And in any case, this is all still hypothetical. If I have real suspicions I shouldn't be talking to you about them. After all, you may have done it." She didn't smile.

"Hey, my alibi checks out, remember?"

"But you're a very clever man, Doctor Connor. And one who provokes considerable loyalty, I suspect."

"I thought you couldn't share your suspicions with me."

Kelly looked right into his bright blue eyes. "Touché!" *I wonder how much older than me he is. About ten years? He looks good on it.* "OK, what about motive then? Jealousy, financial gain, religious zealotry or an affair of the heart – the latter being a euphemism we use for shagging." Joseph looked a little embarrassed. "Sorry. I mean, was Doctor Whickham involved with anyone?"

"No, he wasn't. Well, not that I know of. Alec was always quite private about his relationships with women."

"Any with men?"

"Again, not that I'm aware of. I can't help feeling that the arrangement of Alec's body, the shellfish; they all seem to be aimed at making a point."

"What point?"

"Well, that's just it. I don't know. But it would seem that whoever did it wanted to make it look like it had something to do with the remains and Alec's work on them." Joseph paused and looked sheepish again.

"Is there something else you want to tell me?" asked Kelly.

"We found a recent paper Alec had written about his theories on human evolution."

She looked at him over her coffee. "We? Found?"

"My colleague, Mike Osewe, and I found this paper while we were looking for the blog postings. Sorry, but this is part of the earlier offence so you'll forgive me if I don't feel guilty all over again. We did only hack in the once."

"Go on."

"The thing is, the paper doesn't read like it's all Alec's work. It's like his writing style in places, but it doesn't sound like Alec all the way through. More like a collaboration. But there are no other attributions on the paper. He's the only named author. Here, see." He pushed the paper across the table to Kelly and took a large gulp of his coffee. She glanced at the attribution line.

"Well it's a bit thin for a murder motive, but I'll bear it in mind." At that moment her mobile started to vibrate, gyrating across the table. "Sorry, excuse me a minute." She picked it up.

Robson's voice crackled over the poor connection. "We've got some news on the blog postings."

"Well done, that was quick."

"Well, we've made some progress. The blog provider gave me the IP addresses for those comments, so I called the IT guys at the university to see if they meant anything to them. Get this. All four comments were made from university computers, in the Humanities Faculty library. They can't tell exactly which computers they came from, but they do have the records of who was logged onto computers in that library at all four of those times and dates. So, we have the names of two students and one member of staff. "

"I'm coming back now. We need to see these people quick."

"Sure do."

She rang off and turned to Joseph. "I've got to go. It seems your blog postings came from the university."

"Who from?"

She stood up. "I don't know. And I wouldn't tell you if I did. Thanks for the coffee and the chat. I'll be in touch, Doctor Connor."

11

Kelly met Robson outside the university's main entrance. "OK, who have we got as the phantom bloggers then?"

"A couple of American students studying geo-something. A Jo Delgado and a Grant Franklin. Oh, and you'll love this, a divinity lecturer. Doctor Luke Thackray."

"No prizes for guessing which of those I want to see first."

"The good doctor is in the divinity department. It's in the building just round the corner. Follow the signs to the humanities faculty they said. The two students are researchers, apparently, so they're staying in residences here."

Kelly nodded. "OK, let's see if we can track down the Doc first."

They walked around the side of the building into the teeth of a swirling wind that eddied around the courtyard. Just at that moment the sun came out from behind a cloud, dazzling them with the sheer, astonishing joy of the sight that met them. It was an exquisite garden. At its heart was a large chestnut tree in the centre of an immaculate lawn, surrounded by spring flowers that created a riot of colour in the borders; daffodils, hyacinths, polyanthus and forsythia blazed yellow, pink and orange, framing the lawn in a ring of fire. It had been the garden for the inmates of the old hospital when it was still a mental institution in the late 1800s, and the benches around the edges of the lawn were all dedicated to past philanthropists who had made donations to the hospital; a form of insurance for their immortal souls.

Kelly and Robson both felt the uplift to their souls too, and smiled involuntarily. They walked up to the door marked "Humanities Faculty" and pressed the buzzer on the door control.

"Yes?" came a disembodied voice.

"Police, could you let us in please?" The door clicked open.

Kelly walked to the reception desk, took out her ID and asked the receptionist to contact Doctor Thackray, while Robson walked over to the notice board that covered most of one wall of the waiting area. He scanned the flyers and notices. Language courses; help for student finances; art exhibitions; a meditation group. The typical ponsy stuff, he thought. He'd missed the chance of a university place by one 'A' level and had decided to apply directly to join the police at the age of nineteen. Now in his early forties, he'd begun to notice a greying hairline, a little less comfort on the waistband of his trousers and an increasing tendency towards sour grapes. *All signs of ageing, apparently. Isn't there a cream for that?*

Kelly walked back to him. "He's not here but they have his home address. Let's go."

They walked out of the building and back through the glorious garden to Robson's car. "OK, where are we going?"

"Fifty-three Church Road," Kelly replied.

"This just keeps getting better."

Church Road contained an eclectic mix of houses, spanning High Gothic to Arts and Crafts. They cruised down the road looking for Thackray's house, past black and white timber frame frontages and herringbone brick detail. Then they saw number fifty-three and Robson parked right outside.

Thackray's house occupied a space, physically if not stylistically, between a typically Victorian detached house and an Arts and Crafts villa. All the houses on this side of the road were accessed by steps up through their well-kept front gardens, but the garden visible through the wrought iron gate of number fifty-three was just a few remnants of an old lawn and a sad-looking contorted willow bush. A brick wall about nine feet high abutted the pavement and access to the house was via one of two gateways. One had the wrought iron gate set into it, but the other was protected by a studded wooden door that looked more like it belonged in the porch of a medieval manor house. There were two replica arrow slits between the gates and short, spiked railings protruded from the top of the wall.

They could see through the wrought iron gate that the building itself was of a bizarre design, resembling a castle keep more than a family house. It was two windows wide all round and four storeys high, with a flat roof and thick chimney breasts that ran right up both side walls to terminate as wide chimneys. The house was built with brick of a dark ginger colour; the bay window surround to the right of the front door was of cream stone and retained the original timber-framed, outward-opening casements windows. The second, third and fourth floor windows had stone surrounds to the original wooden sash windows, under curved decorative brickwork features in herringbone bond. The front door was unusually wide; large and traditionally panelled, it showed signs of many coats of wood stain. The name "Panolbion" was carved into an ornate stone lintel over the front door.

They got out of the car and as they surveyed the building the warm feeling generated by the Humanities faculty garden began to fade. Kelly murmured, "Arts and Crafts, with more than a tinge of paranoia".

"What?"

"Arts and crafts movement. Late nineteenth, early twentieth century?" Robson looked blank. "Never mind", she said. *I could get used to working with Joseph Connor.*

"No car outside the house. He might not be in," said Robson.

"Or he might not have a car," Kelly replied. "So, which deadly portal gives access to this place of doom, do you reckon?"

Robson walked up to the wrought iron gate and pushed it. It was locked. He tried the wooden door but with the same result. "How the hell do you get up to this house?"

"I think the idea is that you don't," Kelly replied. Then she spotted a large metal rose to the left of the wooden door with a button in the centre. She pressed it. They didn't hear a bell, so just stood there waiting and thinking what to do next. Kelly was just about to delve in her bag for her phone when a clean-shaven, balding man opened the front door and walked down the garden steps to the wrought iron gate. He peered through. "Yes?"

"Doctor Luke Thackray?"

"Yes. Can I help you?"

"Police," said Kelly, as she and Robson showed their ID cards. "We're investigating the death of Doctor Alec Whickham and we'd like to talk to you. May we come in?"

"Oh, yes, of course. I heard about that. Terrible business but I'm not sure how I can help you." He made no move to open the gate.

Kelly tried again. "Could we come in and talk to you please? It won't take long."

Thackray unbolted the gate and showed them up the steps to the house and then into the hallway. He smiled thinly as he turned and directed them into the front parlour. The room smelled old; musty, with overtones of furniture polish and tobacco smoke. And it felt profoundly cold. There were four chairs and a dark wooden table in the window bay, a dark wooden dresser against one of the walls and three large leather armchairs around an open fire grate. The grate showed no sign of a fire having been lit for some time and there was no other obvious form of heating in the room. Kelly shivered a little, partly due to the low temperature but also because the room had a feeling of death about it. She could imagine generations of house owners and their families being laid out here, in the 'best room'. The only thing missing was an aspidistra.

"Please, sit down. Would you like some afternoon tea? Or a coffee?"

"No, thank you, I've just had one," Kelly replied, before Robson was able to say anything. He shot her a look. "I'm Detective Inspector Kelly and this is my colleague, DS Robson. As I said, we're investigating the death of Doctor Alec Whickham and we'd like to talk to you about some postings that appeared on his blog a couple of weeks before he died. They seem to have been posted by someone who has strong feelings about evolutionary theory. Do you know anything about this?"

Thackray shook his head. "Nothing at all. I don't even know what a blog is. I've heard of them, but that's all."

"I have to ask you this, Doctor Thackray. Where were you on the evening of the tenth of April?"

"Erm, oh, that was last Tuesday wasn't it? It was the day of the parish council meeting, which I attended. It began at eight o'clock and finished at around nine."

"Can anyone verify your movements that evening?"

"Well, the members of the parish council certainly can until nine o'clock, but after that I'm afraid I was alone here."

"No Mrs Thackray?" asked Robson.

"Alas, no. My wife died five years ago. She was killed in a road accident, whilst riding her bicycle. The roads are really too dangerous these days. Very overcrowded."

"I'm sorry," said Kelly. "I expect that's put you off cycling for life."

"Well, yes, it has I'm afraid. I did have a bicycle, but ... well, after my wife died I lost the enthusiasm for riding. I walk a great deal now and use public transport."

"You don't drive, then?" asked Robson.

"No. Strange as it may sound in this day and age, I have never learned to drive. I never really saw the need to." Thackray's brow furrowed. " But I'm sure you haven't come here to talk about my modes of transport. How can I help you about Doctor Whickham?"

"What is your opinion on evolution, Doctor Thackray?" asked Kelly.

A cloud passed over his face. "Heretical claptrap."

"Did you ever discuss this with Alec Whickham?"

"No. I never met the man."

"But you knew about his work?"

"One could hardly escape it these past weeks. It's been all over the local and national news, and the university has been crowing about it at every opportunity. Doctor Whickham seemed to be a very dedicated man, but ultimately misguided in my view. I would never wish him harm, though."

Kelly smiled. "I wonder if I could change my mind about that cup of tea?"

Thackray was momentarily taken aback. "Oh, of course. And you Sergeant?" he asked, turning to Robson.

"Yeah, white with two sugars thanks."

"And how do you take yours, Inspector?" he asked, rising from his chair.

"Black, no sugar please".

"I'll make a pot then." Thackray walked out of the room.

"Why the tea?" whispered Robson.

"We need some time with this guy. There's something ... I just want more time to talk with him and I need to think first."

Robson took the hint and didn't reply. He looked around the room. The wallpaper was old anaglypta that had been buried under many coats of emulsion. It was now a dark cream colour and the paintwork was not much brighter. The ceiling was also stained with light brown patches, and the smell of old pipe tobacco was unmistakable. Bookshelves obscured two of the walls, but on the wall opposite the window was a large picture of a medieval monk. It looked like a stained glass window.

"He looks a bit worried about something," said Robson.

"I think I've offended him," Kelly replied.

"No, the monk in that picture." Robson got up from the creaking leather chair and walked over to take a closer look at it. As he got near the dresser he noticed two dried dark spots on the wooden floor. He bent down and rubbed at them. They were reddish brown. "Hey, I think this might be blood." Then he heard Thackray rattling back down the hall with a tea tray. Robson straightened up quickly and looked intently at the painting, just as Thackray came through the door.

"He's William of Ockham. Quite a hero of mine," said Thackray, putting the tray down on the large table. "A Franciscan friar and great thinker and philosopher of the fourteenth century. The picture is a reproduction of a recent stained glass window in All Saints Church at Ockham in Surrey. I wrote a biography of William in 1999 and the local historical society very kindly presented me with the picture when the window was completed a few years ago. You have heard of Occam's razor?"

"I'm a Gillette man myself," said Robson under his breath. Thackray either didn't hear him or chose to ignore him. He poured the tea.

"Simple is best, as I understand it?" said Kelly.

"An effective application of the razor to its own definition, Inspector. The principle is more commonly stated that when there are two competing theories that make exactly the same prediction, the simpler one is the better. More correctly, it's the application of the law of parsimony; that entities should not be multiplied unnecessarily. Although William never actually wrote the razor down, it's a principle which pervades much of his writing. Of course, he borrowed heavily from Aristotle and many other philosophers down the ages, and the principle was commonly applied in the medieval period. So he didn't invent it, as it were. But he did develop it very astutely. It's the principle that guides my belief in creationism. Evolution seems to me to be simply too complex and unlikely. Why strive for a more complicated explanation when we have the truth staring us in the face? We don't need anything else but God. We can use the razor to shave away all other explanations."

As he passed a cup to Kelly she noticed a plaster showing through his shirt sleeve.

"Have you hurt yourself, Doctor Thackray?"

He looked down at his arm. "Oh, yes, I cut myself." He turned to Robson. "I'll leave you to put in your own sugar."

"Do any of your colleagues share your belief in creationism?" asked Kelly, as Thackray sat back down in his armchair.

"There is a small group of us. Just half a dozen or so. We meet up every now and then, but it isn't anything formal."

"I'd like the names of the people in that group, please."

His irritation was evident as he got up and went to the dresser, opened a top drawer and took out a sheet of paper and a pen. Kelly sipped her tea whilst Robson downed his in one and got himself a refill. Thackray wrote the names of the creationist group regulars on a sheet of paper and handed it to Kelly. "I am quite sure that none of them are murderers."

"I've no wish to offend you. I simply have a job to do." She took the paper and handed it on to Robson. "By the way, do you use the computers in the Humanities Faculty library?"

"On occasions, yes."

"And you are sure that you have not used them to comment on Doctor Whickham's blog?"

"No. As I say, I don't really understand what a blog is. I haven't written anything about Doctor Whickham's work anywhere. Why do you think I had anything to do with it?"

"The university's IT records show you as being logged into the computers there at all the times and dates when the blog comments were made. Can you explain that?" asked Robson.

Thackray looked blank. "No, I'm afraid I can't. It may simply be a coincidence. I can assure you that I have not made any public comments on any of Doctor Whickham's work. I wouldn't know how to comment on a blog, in any case."

"How long have you been lecturing Divinity?" asked Kelly, looking for a way to keep him talking. She just couldn't get a handle on the man.

"All my working life. I studied at Oxford and then began teaching there. After six years I left and moved back here to teach at the local school, and then I moved to the university twenty-three years ago. Of course, it was the polytechnic then."

"This is a very ... unusual house," said Kelly, struggling for the right word.

Thackray smiled unconvincingly. "Yes indeed, it is rather eccentric, I suppose. It was built by my great grandfather in 1885. My family has provided the vicars of this parish for three generations. It was the vicarage until 1960 when the parish combined with its neighbour, Durdley. The vicar of Durdley parish church became the vicar of this parish too. My father lost his position and, rather than move, he took the position of divinity teacher at St Thomas Aquinas private school, just next to the church here. I have followed in his footsteps as far as teaching divinity is concerned, but not into the priesthood. Being the youngest meant that I didn't face any particular pressure to follow the family tradition. I was able to do it because I wanted to. My eldest brother had to rebel, as the greatest expectation fell on him, of course."

"What did he do?"

"He studied archaeology, in point of fact. A strange coincidence under the present circumstances. He's seventeen years older than me and is now retired, however."

Kelly judged that they had probably got as far as they were going to at this interview, and she was running out of ideas to keep him talking. She looked at her watch. "Well, thank you for your time Doctor

Thackray. We may need to be in touch with you again."

He stood up. "To eliminate me from your enquiries, as the saying goes?" There was a sarcastic edge to his voice.

Kelly stood up too, and smiled briefly. "Something like that. Thank you for the tea."

Thackray led them out of the house and down the steps to the wooden door in the front wall. Kelly and Robson walked through and turned to say good bye, but he had already closed the gate behind them with a clunk and they could hear the bolt being drawn across the lock. They walked back to the car.

"What do you make of him?" asked Robson.

"I really don't know, but there's a lot more we'll need to talk to Doctor Thackray about. I'm sure of that."

"So, what next?"

"Don't know that either. I've got some ideas but I need to let them ferment for a while."

"Are you dropping a hint that you need a drink?"

"There you are, you see," said Kelly, opening the car door. "You're not that daft after all."

12

Mike swiped his ID card through the door control to the outer office of lab G012 and he and Joseph went in. It was the first time Joseph had been back to the lab since finding Alec dead, and he hadn't been looking forward to it. Mike hadn't been there since before Alec's death, but he too felt the emotion of being in the place where Alec had died. They walked towards the lab door and stopped just outside it; they looked at each other, silent and uneasy. Joseph nodded to Mike and he swiped his card again. The lab door slid open.

Joseph noticed that the smell had changed, which was a relief. The metallic tinge had gone and the more familiar, dry bone and dust smell had returned. He walked over to where the two trolleys had stood. Now there was just one. Nimue lay there, with the fossilized mussels still placed around her head. Mike followed him over to the trolley. "Wow. God. Amazing! No wonder Alec was so excited about this," he whispered.

Joseph nodded. "She is pretty fantastic, isn't she? And why are you whispering?"

Mike smiled. "I've no idea," he said, in a normal voice. "I guess she gives me a feeling of …" He frowned and shrugged, unable to express it.

"Reverence," said Joseph.

"Yeah, that's exactly it..." His voice became quieter again. "Reverence."

"I didn't get much chance to see her last time I was here," Joseph said, with sadness in his voice. "But now I do, I envy you working on her. Even though she is quite a jigsaw puzzle in places." He pulled on a pair of fine gloves and carefully picked up part of the pelvis. He turned it round in his fingers. "She's amazingly complete."

Mike looked over the pieces carefully. "Yeah, and Alec and his team have done a good job in the reconstruction so far." He put a pair of gloves on and picked up part of an ulna. He stared at it, transfixed.

"Are you OK?" asked Joseph.

"I'm fine. I think the astonishment of knowing I have the responsibility of leading this has hit home. I nearly fell over when the VC called me at the weekend and told me that the Kenyan authorities had made it a condition that I direct the project if she's to remain here for the planned four months. I guess it's because my mum is Kenyan and worked for the National Museums. I'm dead excited, but truthfully, pretty nervous."

"You've got Alec's team working with you though. He always rated them highly."

"Yeah, that's true. Oh, I'm really chuffed to get this opportunity, don't get me wrong. It's just the responsibility."

"You don't like responsibility, do you?" asked Joseph. It sounded a bit hard, harder than he meant it to, but he let it stand. Mike didn't seem offended.

"No, that's true. Never have. Still, it's what's coming my way now, so I'll need to buckle down and get used to it."

Joseph smiled. "I'll let you get started then. I expect minute by minute updates, remember!"

Mike smiled back as Joseph walked towards the lab door, pulling off his gloves and throwing them into the nearby bin.

"Joe?"

He turned round. "Yeah?"

Mike looked like he was about to say something, but then changed his mind. "Wish me luck!"

"You won't need it. Can't think of anyone more capable of doing this." The door slid open and Joseph left.

Mike looked back at the skeleton lying in front of him. He picked up the skull and looked at it closely. Distinct brow ridges; two clear ridges running from the tops of the eye sockets across the crown; *yep, looks like Homo ergaster alright*. He turned it round to inspect the back, expecting to see the familiar anterior ridge. But that isn't what he saw.

Joseph had just got back into his office when his phone rang.

"Joe, get back down here quick!" It was Mike.

"What's happened?" he asked.

"Just come down now. You have to see this."

"OK." He put the phone down with a sickening sense of déjà vu. Mike sounded exactly as Alec had done on the evening he died. Joseph almost ran out of the office and down the stairs to the lab block. He swiped his card and walked into the lab to see Mike holding the skull and looking at it with disbelief. He held it out to Joseph, back first.

"Get some gloves back on and look at this."

Joseph obeyed, took hold of the skull and immediately saw that there was a hole in the rear, at the base. It was wider at the centre than at the edges and the bone around the edges of the hole showed signs of radiating hairline fractures. Even though he was not a human anatomy expert, Joseph could immediately see what it was. "Good God! It's a wound."

"Yeah, and look at where it is. And its shape. Watch this." Mike retrieved the skull from Joseph and picked up the hand axe that had been found next to Nimue. He pushed the point into the hole. It fitted very convincingly.

"That's incredible. She was killed with this hand axe?"

"I'd bet a reasonable amount of money on it. Or at least that she was badly injured and died in the water as a result. She wouldn't have stayed conscious very long with an injury like this. But the really weird thing is that it's the same kind of injury that killed Alec."

"Yeah, it certainly looks like it," said Joseph. "This must have been what Alec was so excited about. It couldn't be the reason he was killed, could it?" Both men looked at each other with apprehension, and then Joseph shook his head. "No, what on earth for? What kind of motive would that be?"

"I don't know. But I'm getting increasingly jittery about this whole fucking thing!" Mike put the skull and axe back on the trolley and leaned on the bench behind him. "What do we do? Should we tell anyone? Does it matter?"

"We probably ought to tell the police. They didn't touch the skeleton when they investigated the accident here. They were only interested in Alec. They did look at the hand axe after I suggested to Kelly that it could be the kind of weapon that was used on Alec, but apparently they didn't find any traces of blood or anything."

"I'm also having another awful thought. How many people knew about the wound to this skull?"

"I don't know. I guess Ben, Lily or Egraine might have known, but knowing Alec I'd say he probably didn't tell anyone. He mostly worked alone and was pretty defensive about his own pet bits of projects. I know he was working on Nimue's skull in his office and wouldn't let anyone in to see it."

"He could have told Juliet," said Mike with a wince.

"Yes, he could indeed. Maybe in the heat of one of their arguments. But actually I don't think it's likely."

"Well, Alec was famous for keeping things to himself," said Mike.

Joseph sat down on one of the lab stools. "True, but someone did know a lot about Alec's views on human evolution, and worked closely with him."

Mike looked surprised. "Who?"

"I don't know, that's the problem."

Mike looked confused. "You're losing me."

"Remember that paper we found on his network drive?"

Mike nodded.

Joseph sighed. "Well, I read it over the weekend and it's ... unexpected."

"How?"

"It's well-balanced, based on evidence and doesn't make any really wild claims."

Mike laughed. "Very unexpected!"

Joseph smiled. "Yeah, exactly." He looked thoughtful.

"So," said Mike, "you'd better tell me what it says. It's obviously eating you up."

"It's just disturbing when you think you know someone. Maybe I didn't. Maybe no one really did."

"Come on, tell me."

"Well, it concentrates so much on language and brain development. He makes the point that language comes at a price. The developments that are necessary in the brain to enable speech also mean that humans suffer from a unique range of mental disabilities ... like autism."

Mike raised his eyebrows.

Joseph nodded and then went on. "And schizophrenia, both of which are connected to problems in areas of the brain that relate to language, particularly the connections between the right and left sides, according to some researchers. They've shown that schizophrenia manifests itself in the same way in all cultures. It appears to be a basic human trait, and it's therefore at least possible that it was manifest in some form in our earlier ancestors as the brain developed to accommodate advances in language. Language must, therefore, have conferred a significant advantage to make it worth the disabilities that accompany it."

"OK, I'm convinced. That line of argument doesn't sound like Alec. Not his area of interest or expertise."

"Yeah. There are other things in the paper, but you get the gist?" He walked towards the lab door.

"Mm, I think I'm beginning to" said Mike. "Can I get a copy and read it?"

"Sure."

As Mike followed Joseph out of the lab he took one last look at Nimue. "Y'know, I get the oddest feeling when I look at her."

Joseph turned around. "Nimue?"

"Yeah."

"What feeling?"

"Can't explain it," said Mike. "Like she's trying to say something." He switched off the lab lights. "Ignore me. I'm just going bonkers."

Joseph laughed as they stepped through the doorway and the glass door slid closed behind them. "Maybe you can help her to tell her story."

"I hope so."

They switched off the remaining lights and left the lab, dark and still. Nimue lay on the table, smiling.

13

Kelly's mobile played a tinny version of Peter Gabriel's Solsbury Hill. She saw the call was from Joseph Connor, and felt a little surge of excitement. *Oh for God's sake woman, grow up.* She flipped it open. "Doctor Connor, how are you?"

"Dazed and confused."

Kelly recognised the Led Zeppelin allusion. "Hey, hey, what can I do?"

Joseph laughed. "Mike Osewe and I have just been down to the lab to start work on Nimue, and Mike found something we think might be relevant."

"What's that?"

"Alec finished reconstructing the skull just before he died. He was really excited about something and asked me to go down to see it, like I told you. Well, I think I know what he was excited about. There's a wound at the back of the skull, near the base. Weirdly, it's in what looks like the same place as the wound to Alec's head. And it's shaped like a ... a ..."

"Don't tell me. Pointed wedge," said Kelly.

"Exactly. So, we tried fitting the hand axe that was found with her into the hole, and it's a pretty good fit."

"So you're telling me that Nimue and Alec Whickham were killed in the same way?"

"Well, we couldn't swear to it as we haven't seen the wound to Alec's head in any detail, but it sounds strikingly similar. I don't know if it means anything, but we thought we'd better tell you."

"Who knew about this?" asked Kelly.

"We've been asking ourselves the same question, and we don't know. Alec didn't say what he wanted to show me when he called, and we don't know how much his research team knew. I guess you'll need to ask them."

"Would Professor Bailey have known?"

"Again, I don't know."

"OK, well, thanks for letting me know. I'll need to ask the pathologist to take a look at the skull and compare the wounds, so I'd be grateful if you didn't do any more on the skull."

"Sure, there's plenty more for Mike to work on."

There was indeed plenty more and Mike got down to it immediately. He was on a tight schedule, he realised that, so he called a meeting with Lily, Ben and Egraine the next day. And he couldn't help himself; he had to ask them if they knew about Nimue's skull. But they appeared completely taken by surprise by what Mike told them. They confirmed that Alec had worked on the skull himself, and had been very secretive about it. They all had their own particular areas to work on, and knew better than to ask Alec how his work was going.

Later that evening Mike called Sophie to let her know that he'd be late home, and then went back down to the lab by himself. He looked down at Nimue's skull on the table, trying to imagine how she might have looked when she was alive. "Who were you?" he whispered. "And who killed you?" The skull gaped back. "Let's see if you can at least tell me the answer to the first question," he murmured as he put on a pair of fine lab gloves and picked up the skull.

14

The hearse moved slowly along the street, followed by a cortege of seven cars, and turned into the driveway of Woodland Memories. Alec had been very clear about his funeral wishes in his will. The celebration of his life was to be humanist and he wished to be buried, not cremated. As he had gained so much in his life from examining human remains, he very much wanted to remain a potential part of that activity after his death. There was also something about being burned that he found instinctively repellent. As a staunch environmentalist, he had willed to be buried wrapped in a recycled paper shroud, near or amongst the roots of a tree. Woodland Memories offered exactly that service, as their cemetery was a tract of managed woodland fertilised, very effectively, by their clients. Or 'guests' as Mr Symonds, the proprietor, was wont to call them.

The cause of death had definitely been established as a blow to the back of his head with a sharp, heavy object and all toxicology reports had come back negative. So, the Police had released Alec's body for burial and his parents had organised the funeral near to his adopted home on the Lancashire coast, largely so that as many as possible of his colleagues and friends could attend easily. His mother was afraid that his funeral would be poorly attended as he had few real friends. But they also chose the area because of Woodland Memories. The cemetery was a beautiful place, there was no denying it. Although the proprietor could be overwhelmingly syrupy, the cemetery was well run and had impeccable environmental credentials. In particular it catered for humanist funerals so the arrangements had been easy. But not cheap.

In place of a religious service, the group of family and friends invited to the interment gathered in the small chapel to remember Alec's life, to say goodbye to him and to pay their respects for a life so tragically cut short. The congregation was by invitation and included just Alec's immediate family and close friends, including Joseph and Anna. Everyone had the opportunity to say something to the small group of mourners, and Alec's mother was determined to do this, despite the emotional toll she knew it would take. Shaking, and almost overcome with grief, she took her turn to stand in front of her son's coffin. Her husband and two sons supported her, as her husband whispered, "You don't have to do this Ellen. Everyone will understand."

She pulled herself up, gave him a squeeze on the arm and turned to face the group. "Alec loved what he did. Even when he was very young he used to show me all the things he'd collected on the beach when we went on holiday. He could be difficult, I know. But he was good, right the way through. He was my beautiful boy." Tears welled up and she broke down, sobbing. Her husband and sons led her back to her chair and helped her to sit down.

As the congregation filed out of the chapel and into warm spring sunshine, Alec's coffin was prepared to be driven out to the woodland. His body had been in a coffin for the duration of the service, but it would need to be removed and placed in its paper shroud at the burial site. This wasn't considered appropriate viewing for family and friends, so they had said their final goodbyes in the chapel. Alec's parents had booked a local hotel for the buffet lunch at one pm, and opened the invitation to attend to anyone from the university. As the mourners walked back to the car park, they passed the wishing well, most of them stopping to throw in some coins.

Kelly and Robson had been invited to the buffet too, and as usual Robson had the job of driving. Kelly always felt that being driven around was one of the few perks of being a senior officer. As he drove towards the hotel, Robson caught sight of a woman standing across the road from the car park entrance. She was wearing high heeled boots with an ankle-length great coat and a dark scarf over her hair. Robson knew her, he was sure, but just couldn't remember where from. He turned to Kelly. "That woman over there, I'm sure I know her from somewhere. Do you recognise her?"

Kelly looked. "No, doesn't look familiar. And I'd be happier if you stopped eyeing up the local talent and kept your eyes on the road." He parked and got out of the car, but when he looked over again, she had gone.

By the time the funeral group reached the hotel a number of people from the university were already there; the Vice Chancellor and his wife and a couple of the deans who had known Alec and taken an interest in his work. None of his old colleagues from Birmingham had come, though. Juliet hadn't come either, as she felt too awkward to meet Alec's parents, but had sent flowers and a message saying that she would be thinking about the Whickhams at their time of loss and assuring them that she always had the greatest regard for Alec. It was just as well that Juliet hadn't attended, as Alec's mother had torn up her card and put the flowers into the nearest waste bin as soon as she had seen them at the cemetery.

Alec's family stood by the door to the main room, accepting the condolences of the people attending with good grace, but also with clear distress. Joseph picked up a glass of wine from a tray offered by one of the waiters and walked into the main room with the rest of the funeral group. Large circular tables had been laid out in the centre of the room and a long buffet ran along the wall at one side, opposite the bay windows that looked out over the Fylde coast.

Anna walked over to the windows to look out across the sand flats that were peppered with wading birds making the most of the low spring tide. The sun sparkled on the sea beyond. "It's a beautiful view from here," she said, turning to Joseph who had followed her across the room.

"It is."

"I wonder how many people will come. I do hope Alec's family aren't embarrassed on top of the grief."

Joseph turned back to look at the room. "It looks like a reasonable turn-out, and the VC's come along so that'll make them feel that Alec was appreciated, even if he wasn't very well-liked."

"Joseph!"

"Sorry love, it's just true. I liked him, but a lot of people didn't."

Anna shook her head as she looked back across the sand flats to the sea. "Well someone didn't like him one bit, or we wouldn't all be here today."

The hotel staff began taking the covers off the cold part of the buffet whilst two servers took up their positions behind the hot plates. A queue formed quickly and everyone shuffled along it, making their food choices. After they had filled their plates, Joseph and Anna looked for somewhere to sit. Mike was at a table with Ben, Lily and Egraine. A man in a clerical collar was just sitting down with them. "Shall we sit with Mike?" asked Joseph.

"Oh yes, I haven't had chance to ask him how Sophie's feeling now," answered Anna.

They walked over to the table and Mike stood up to give Anna a kiss and a hug. "Sophie can't make it. She's still feeling pretty awful," he said, before Anna had a chance to ask.

"Oh dear. Please give her my love won't you. If there's anything I can do to help, please tell her to call me anytime." Mike smiled and nodded as they all sat down at the table.

Joseph introduced Anna to Alec's researchers and then turned to the cleric. "I'm so sorry, I don't think we've met."

"Ah, no, I'm Jim Whickham. Alec's cousin."

"Hello." They shook hands. "I'm Joseph Connor. I worked closely with Alec for a number of years. This my wife Anna."

Jim leaned over and shook hands. "Delighted to meet you."

"I'm so very sorry for your loss" said Anna, trying to unwrap her knife and fork from the complicated folds of the serviette.

"Thank you, yes. It was a terrible shock, although I have to admit that I didn't know Alec very well, I'm ashamed to say. On the occasions when we did meet, we didn't ... er ... see eye to eye, I'm afraid.
"

"It's a shame when families drift apart," said Joseph. *A dreadful platitude, but what can you say?*

"Oh, it wasn't really a drift. I would call it more a split. I always wanted to enter into a discussion with Alec about evolution from the perspective of a creationist like myself, but unfortunately he would never engage with the conversation. I was always sorry that I couldn't discuss these issues with someone of Alec's obvious intellect." Jim set about trying to release his own cutlery from its serviette cocoon.

"What were the issues you wanted to air with Alec?" asked Mike, glancing over at Joseph who raised his eyebrows a little. They were both thinking about the comments on Alec's blog.

"Oh well, how can humans have evolved such profound understanding? How could evolution result in a creature that can comprehend the meaning of a god? Can we evolve souls, and if so, how do we live in this world to protect our souls in the next?" said Jim. Nobody moved. "Sorry," he said, smiling to break the weight of the moment. "That must sound like quite a list!"

"Well, Alec was a confirmed atheist, so he probably wouldn't have seen the purpose of the conversation, I'm afraid," replied Joseph.

Jim nodded. "Very true." He started work on his vol au vent. "Do you have any thoughts on the matter, Doctor Connor?" he asked.

"I don't believe in a traditional Christian god, I just can't. The evidence of the world around me doesn't back it up. But, I don't know about a god who plays dice. I'm an agnostic when it comes to that kind of god," said Joseph.

"Why?" asked Jim.

"Well, by application of scientific process, I suppose. I can neither prove nor disprove the existence of a god that sets up the rules and then lets the game play with no intervention. I can't gather any evidence either way, so I can't take a position on it. I guess I'm saying that I'm an atheist in relation to some gods and an agnostic in relation to others!" said Joseph.

"But isn't it taking the Bible literally that gives Christians the real problem?" asked Mike. "My sense has always been that belief in a god per se isn't too much of a problem for evolutionary theory. As Joseph says, you can imagine a god that sets the rules up and then lets the game run. Evolution is then just the mechanism by which the game progresses. It's biblical doctrine that's the problem, isn't it?"

Jim smiled. "Ah, yes. The argument that science just enables us to hear God thinking. I have to admit that I do find some credibility in that view, but I still struggle with some aspects of evolutionary theory from a more theoretical point of view. I can see the similarities between humans and apes, but nothing in the theory that satisfactorily accounts for the differences. The simplest explanation is that we have been chosen by God. All uncertainties dissolve in the face of that understanding."

Mike leaned across the table. "You know, that's always been something I haven't understood about creationism. If you believe that God created the world as it says in the Bible, and that the Flood was real, for example, why would you want to try to give scientific explanations for it too? Surely that defeats the point you are making that God created everything. It seems you want to have both explanations work at the same time. I mean why do you need a swarm of comets dumping water on the earth if God simply willed it?" Mike looked hard to see if the last part of his little speech provoked any reaction. But, there was nothing.

"Actually, to me evidence is irrelevant," said Lily. "I do believe in God and I work as a scientist. I don't see any conflict. My spiritual beliefs don't come from the same place as my belief in science and I don't feel the need to reconcile the two. As Doctor Osewe says, we're probably uncovering the way God works. That was what Newton believed he was doing, wasn't it? It's no big deal to me if the people who wrote the Bible got some of it wrong. They were human after all."

"Yeah, but any god gives you a problem with evolution," said Ben. "If all things evolve, where did God evolve from? What came before God? Who or what created him or her? All religions end up with this problem and so they turn to creationism. The belief in a god means you can't pursue proper science."

Mike put his knife and fork down hard on the table. "Whoa, a massively simplistic overstatement, Ben. Islam doesn't have anything like the same problem with evolution as Christianity does. I was brought up in Kenya, a very Christian country, but my mother was a Muslim, although somewhat lapsed towards the end of her life. Creationism is a very Christian phenomenon, and it's just another example of how the doctrine of the Bible being taken literally precludes an open mind and leads to the suppression of science and scientists. You have to admit that Christianity has a pretty poor record on its treatment of scientists, with respect Reverend Whickham." Jim nodded curtly. "Yet from the way things are reported in the press these days, we get the impression that Islam is a fundamentalist, repressive religion. In relation to science and technology that just isn't the case. There isn't really any contradiction between the Qu'ran and the theory of evolution as far as I know. And, an Islamic scholar in the mid eighteenth century wrote that between animals and men there are monkeys[4]. That predates Darwin by a hundred years."

"You make a good point," said Jim, trying to appear reasonable but given away by the deepening furrows in his brow. "But my question about the apparently planned nature of life still remains."

"It was probably worked out by Arabic scholars two thousand years ago, but is buried in some texts somewhere that no one west of Turkey can be bothered to read!" said Mike, getting up and walking back towards the buffet table. Egraine

---

[4] Quote from the Islamic scholar Ibrahim Hakki Erzurumi (1703 – 1780). He lived in Erzurum, now in the Republic of Turkey. He is most famous for his encyclopaedic work Marifetname, which includes the passage "…between plants and animals there is sponge, and between animals and humans there is monkey". Charles Darwin was born in 1809 and died in 1882.

watched him go, her eyes running down his back and resting on his buttocks. She grinned a little and got up to follow him, leaving the rest of them at the table to smile at each other in vague embarrassment.

Egraine edged up to Mike as they refilled their plates at the buffet. "Doctor Osewe, can I come and see you soon? I know you'll be busy, but I think there's a lot of synergy between your research interests and my research into bone structures in early Homo species. My thesis is on developing more sophisticated classifications between quadripedal and bipedal, which take account of hand development in primates. I wondered if you'd think about supervising my PhD. Alec was my supervisor so it makes sense that you might take over that role now that you're directing the Nimue project. Could I come and see you about it tomorrow?"

"Sure, I'm in tomorrow morning before eleven if you can make it then? You'll need to bring your work so far as I'm not familiar with what you've been doing, but I'm happy to meet up and you can talk me through it. And like I said the other day, call me Mike." He balanced a final chicken wing on top of his piled up plate and walked away from the buffet.

Egraine's eyes settled on his backside again. *I'd call you any time.*

Kelly and Robson walked out of the hotel and into the car park. The woman they had seen before was standing by the gatepost, watching the wake through the large bay windows of the hotel.

"She's there again," said Kelly. "Have you remembered who she is?"

A look of sudden recognition lit his face. "Tammy Walker!" He went over to talk to her but she hurried off before he got near her. "Hey, Tammy, just want a quick word love!"

She broke into a trot and turned the corner at the end of the road without looking back.

"So, who's Tammy Walker?" asked Kelly, as Robson returned to the car, panting hard.

"Local prostitute. Funny kid. Picked her up a few times for soliciting a couple of years ago, but haven't seen anything of her in the last eighteen months."

"What's she doing here then, I wonder? She certainly seemed interested in Doctor Whickham's funeral. Have you got her last known?"

"We should have. I'll check when we get back and then go and pay her a visit."

15

A knock came at the office door.

"Come in," Mike shouted. It was Egraine. Usually she had her hair tied back and wore loose fitting jumpers, but today she was dressed in tight jeans with a low cut top, and her hair was down, falling over her face in light brown waves. A little make up too; some mascara and lip gloss.

"Hi Egraine," said Joseph.

Mike looked up and smiled. He hadn't noticed what a good body she had before now, and then immediately told himself that it was inappropriate to think that. *Inappropriate but, well, still inescapable.*

"Have a seat Egraine. Would you like a tea or coffee?" Mike walked over to the kettle.

"Yes, coffee would be great thanks." She turned to Joseph. "Actually, will this be disturbing for you Doctor Connor?" She looked back to Mike. "We could go to one of the coffee bars. They're still quiet at the moment."

"Yes, good idea," said Mike, before Joseph had time to reply. He picked up his notebook and held the door open for Egraine. As she walked out in front of him, he turned to Joseph and winked. Joseph rolled his eyes in response.

They walked down the corridor and into the Java Man coffee bar. "I'll get these. What would you like?" asked Mike.

"Oh, thank you, I'll have an Americano please." She ran her hand through her hair and smiled as she looked Mike in the eyes just a little longer than normal.

He paid for the coffees and they sat at a corner table by the window.

"So," he said, "tell me about what you're doing."

"I've been working with Alec for the past eighteen months on bone structures in early humans. As we were discussing yesterday, I feel there is too little effective differentiation between forms of locomotion and use of hands, so everything gets lumped together into bipedal or quadripedal. Apes are neither, in my view, and some monkeys and other primates aren't either. To class them all as knuckle-walkers doesn't tell the real story about the subtleties of the relationship between hand manipulation and forms of locomotion. I've been working on a different set of classifications ..." She picked up her bag and began to look through the books and papers. "I've brought some sketches to show you what I mean ...or, at least I thought I did. Oh, how annoying. I was sure I put them in here. I have a set of sketches and some models that I've been putting together from casts of ape and hominin bones. The models are in my flat. I must have left the sketches there too."

As she spoke she leaned forward to look through her bag. Her top was very low cut, and as she looked up she caught Mike looking at her breasts. He quickly raised his eyes, but she had seen his interest and smiled at him again.

"It would be so much easier to show you what I mean rather than try to explain it. We could pop round to my flat just now, if you had the time?"

The surprise of this sudden invitation made him start. "Er, no, I'm afraid I've got a meeting in twenty minutes."

"Oh, shame. How about later? I'm just in Rufus Court, it's only five minutes in the car. I could be there after two o'clock?" Her persistence made it difficult to say no.

"I could make it at about two thirty, then, I suppose. Just for half an hour."

"Great! I'm in flat ten A." She sipped her coffee and leaned back in her chair, running her fingers through her hair. "You said at Alec's funeral that you were brought up in Kenya. Is that where you got interested in palaeontology?"

"Yes, it was. Both my parents worked with the Leakey's at the National Museums of Kenya and I used to go to work with them on occasions and see all the bones and hominin remains. I got fascinated. They come out of the ground like giant jigsaw puzzles and my mum and dad spent hours cleaning them and trying to put them back together."

"Are your mum and dad both from Kenya?" asked Egraine.

"No, dad was from Huddersfield." Mike grinned. "My mum and dad met when mum came over to do a Master's degree in the UK on an exchange studentship. They got married in this country and dad took mum's name as his was Badcock and he was fed up with it, he said." Egraine laughed. "After they were married they went to live in Kenya for a few years to work at the National Museums. They both got research positions in universities here in the UK when I was nine, so we relocated here. I think dad was quite glad to be back living in the UK. The heat in Kenya used to really get to him. But he would never dream of coming back to the UK without mum. They were always inseparable." Mike stirred his coffee. "They even died together."

"Oh, I'm sorry." said Egraine.

"Thanks. It was ten years ago. They were in a pile up on the M6. A foggy and icy night when some tosser in an SUV ran into them. He was driving too close and too fast, the usual thing."

"That must have been dreadful for you. But it sounds like they were a happy and romantic couple."

"Mm, some of the racist intolerance they suffered when they came back from Kenya wasn't very romantic."

"Oh no. Why?"

"A white man married to a black woman, and an intelligent one with a science career too, wasn't very acceptable in the 1980's. Still isn't, if we're honest. Sophie and I get some strange looks sometimes, even now. I got called all kinds of things at school."

Egraine shook her head. "That's dreadful. People can be so ignorant. Well, I agree with your dad. I think Africans are so much more attractive than pale Europeans." She looked at him over the top of her coffee cup.

Mike began to feel that things were moving a bit too fast and that he was being swept along with them. She was clearly attracted to him, and that recognition aroused him. But he knew it shouldn't. He loved Sophie. Things were a bit stressed at the moment and there wasn't much intimacy between them, but that would pass once the baby was born. Hopefully. He abruptly changed the subject.

"So, what about you? How come you're into digging up old bones?"

"I've always been good at the sciences, but was bored by physics and chemistry. It sounds a bit corny, but I went on a school trip to the Natural History Museum one time and loved the dinosaur skeletons. I realised I wanted to do something that involved digging up bones, and then got interested in the debates around human evolution. Mum and dad have lived all over the world; my dad's a diplomatic civil servant. So, on holidays from boarding school I used to go and stay with them in all sorts of exotic places. Africa, Egypt, the Middle East. I didn't have many friends there of course, so I ended up spending a lot of time in museums and reading books."

"Sounds a bit lonely."

Her smile disappeared for a moment, and when it came back it looked painted onto her face. "Well," she said lightly, "it was a great opportunity to see some amazing places."

Mike downed his espresso in one. "Absolutely. Well, sorry Egraine, I have to get going to this meeting."

"Sure, I understand. I'll see you this afternoon at two thirty? Flat ten A, remember."

It was Mike's turn to paint on a smile. "Yes, see you then." He walked out of the coffee bar without looking back. Egraine sat back in her chair watching him go, then caught sight of the guy behind the bar staring at her. She pulled the edge of her top up to cover more of her cleavage and got her jumper out of her bag. Slipping it over her shoulders she tied it with the arms to cover her chest, then scowled at him. He shrugged and turned back to his coffee machine. *Some girls, honestly. They wear hardly any clothes and then get upset when you look.*

16

Jack Robson parked his car on the side of the road, a few hundred yards from Tammy's house. He didn't want to get her into any trouble with her neighbours. In any case, he wasn't sure if she still lived here. This was the last address they had on file, but she hadn't been picked up for soliciting for more than eighteen months. He walked up to the small terraced house and rang the bell. A thin young woman opened the door.

"Hello Tammy. Got a minute for a chat?"

"Oh, shit. You'd better come in."

He followed her down the hall and into a clean but bare kitchen. As she turned round he noticed the yellowing marks of old bruises on her arms.

"How's tricks?" he asked. She shot him a dirty look. "Earning an honest crust now?"

"Look, I don't break any laws Jack. Not now. I just get on with my own business."

"And what business is that?"

"The usual."

"Still on the game then?"

"That's my concern, not yours. Like I say, I don't break any laws."

"Look, I'm not here to nick you. I just want to know what you were doing at Alec Whickham's funeral?"

She shrugged. "He was a punter."

"Do you go to all your clients' funerals?"

"He was a decent guy. I don't meet many of 'em. You were in Vice, you know the score. Weirdos, pathetic guys who can't get it anywhere else. I'm not in this job for the people I meet." She lit a cigarette and threw the pack across the table at him. "Want one?" He shook his head. "Alec was different. Good looking, fit, smart. And dead straight. Just wanted to fuck. Finally I get some job satisfaction." She smiled outwardly, but the pain behind her eyes was clear.

"Did he say anything about his work, the people he met?"

"No, he never said very much at all. But he was a gentleman. OK, I know that's old-fashioned, but he was. Always said thank you. Sweet."

"The last time you saw him before he died, did he seem OK? Did he seem worried about anything?" She shook her head and flicked her cigarette ash into the sink. A tear ran down her cheek. "You were fond of him, weren't you?"

She sniffed and straightened up. "Me? No. I learned a long time ago that I'm not the kind of person people love. Never will be. They just want sex. So, I might as well make some money out of it. Rule one; never get fond of the punters."

"How did he find you? If you're not on the street any more, how do you turn tricks?"

She laughed. "Turn tricks? Get with it, Jack!" She went past him to the kitchen door and beckoned him with a finger. He followed her into the lounge, where she pointed at her computer. "Wonders of modern technology. No more cold nights standing around on the street for me, pet. I'm on the web!"

"So he first contacted you from a website?" She nodded. "Did he come here or did you meet somewhere else?"

"He came here, most Wednesday evenings when he wasn't away on a dig. He didn't come one

Wednesday a few weeks ago and then I saw the report on the local TV the next day."

"And how did you find out about his funeral?"

"Oh, I rang the university. Said I was an old friend from home and had lost the address of the hotel. Having a Geordie accent helped, I guess"

"OK, is there anything else that you can think of that might help us find who killed him? I know helping us isn't something you usually do, but you could make an exception this time."

She looked at Robson hard, as if she were deciding what to say. "I'm saying this for Alec, not for you." She drew hard on her cigarette and blew the smoke out with a long breath, then sat down on the worn sofa. "The day Alec came back from Africa this last time, someone came here and, well, threatened me that I shouldn't see him again. Gave me these bruises into the bargain." She held out her arms.

"What did he look like?"

"He? Yeah, well I guess it was a he. Whoever it was had a raincoat on and a hood up. Just said a few words in a low voice, roughed me up a little bit, and then ran off."

"Can you remember what they said?"

"Not much at all. Just to stay away from Alec Whickham or else. That was it."

"But you did go on seeing him, didn't you? Did this person come back again?"

"Yes. No." She looked at him with contempt and stood up. He realised he had got as much out of her as he was likely to at this visit.

"Why didn't you report this at the time, Tammy? You could have been hurt."

She shrugged. "Occupational hazard."

Robson gave up. "OK, well, thanks for your time." He walked down the hall to the front door.

"Sure you don't fancy a quick one before you go, pet? I might give you a discount, as an old friend." She continued to look at him scornfully.

He opened the front door and turned to see her standing by the lounge door. He looked at her arms. "Get a proper job, love. This is a dangerous game." She gave him a sarcastic smile as he turned back and walked out through the doorway.

"Fuck you Jack, I'm alright!" she shouted as he closed the front door behind him.

Mike knocked on the door of flat ten A, Rufus Court. He wasn't sure why he was here. Part of him knew this was a bad idea, but he rationalised that he had just come to see Egraine's work and if she had a little crush, well, it wouldn't be the first time. He knew how to handle it.

She came to the door. "Thanks for coming Mike. Please come in." She led him down the narrow hall to the lounge at the back of the flat. She had changed out of her jeans and into a short denim skirt. Her long, slim legs were bare and she wore sling-back sandals with two-inch heels. He tried not to look at the way her thighs rippled with every footfall.

On the lounge table were a number of plaster cast models, replica stone artefacts and sketches of ape and human bone structures. "Well, all this looks very impressive," said Mike.

"I hope it all makes sense," she said. "Can I get you something to drink?"

"Just a coffee would be fine, if that's OK?"

"Sure." She disappeared into the small kitchen next to the lounge and switched on the coffee machine, while Mike sat down and started to look at the sketches and models. They really were very good. She came back into the lounge and stood next to him, leaning with her hands on the table. She was so close to him that he could smell her – a light perfume like eau de nil. "These are the sketches I've been making of Nimue. She does have a very human-like skeleton. The pelvis is particularly striking, I think. Narrower than a modern human skeleton, but very clear similarities otherwise." The coffee machine beeped. She brushed her hip against his arm as she turned. "Do you take milk?"

"No, black please."

"My preference too," she replied, with a sensuous smile. She went into the kitchen and came back with two mugs. She put them on the table, and then squatted down next to Mike. "So, what do you think?" she said softly.

"I think there's real promise here."

"No," she said, and then leaned over and kissed him, slowly and fully on the mouth. "I mean what do you think?"

He pulled away from her and stood up quickly. "Egraine, you're very lovely, and a terrible temptation. But ...I can't do this."

He was wavering though, and she could sense it. She moved towards him and held his face in her hands. She kissed him again, this time putting her tongue deep inside his mouth. He couldn't help but respond as she moved one hand down to unzip his jeans and massage his growing erection. He kissed her back hard, pushing up her tight-fitting top and grasping her breasts. She pulled him towards the couch, pushing his jeans and pants down. He was on his knees on the floor as she sat on the couch; she pulled him close. Kissing him deeply she wrapped her legs around him as he moved her thong aside. The act was quick, hard and urgent; pure animal instinct.

"Oh God," he panted as he pulled himself away from her. "I have to go."

She laughed. "But you've only just come!"

He got up off his knees and pulled his jeans up, almost running out of the flat as Egraine lay back, smiling to herself. She heard the door slam. "He'll be back," she said. "Don't you think?"

17

It was late afternoon by the time Robson got back to the station. Kelly looked up as he came towards her desk. "Ma'am?"

"Yeah?"

"Just back from interviewing Tammy Walker."

"Anything interesting?"

"Well, there is certainly a connection. It seems our Doctor Whickham was one of Tammy's regulars."

Kelly raised her eyebrows. "Really? I shouldn't be surprised, I guess. Our job is to ferret out dirty little secrets and we always seem to find them. How long had he been going to her for services, then?"

"No more than eighteen months. She's been advertising on the web and he saw her website. Contacted her first that way. Seems he's been going fairly regularly once a week since then, when he's been in the country." Robson took his jacket off and slung it over the back of his chair at the desk opposite Kelly's. "So she's still on the game, but she's gone online. That's why she dropped off our street-walking radar. But Whickham was a punter, that's for sure. And someone didn't like it." He sat down, opened the fast food bag he'd brought in with him and started to tuck into an enormous burger.

Kelly wrinkled her nose. "Ugh, that smells revolting."

"Mmm, s'great", he said, through a wedge of burger and bun. "Late lunch."

"How do you mean someone didn't like it?"

Robson waved and pointed at his mouth. "Mn a mn mn."

Kelly rolled her eyes. After he swallowed it down, he said, "She was attacked around the time Whickham came back from Africa this last time, and warned to stay away from him. Tammy couldn't tell who it was, she says, but he had a hood up and was tallish. That's all she said." He took another big bite.

"Do you think she's telling the truth?"

Robson nodded. "Remains of big bruises on her arms," he said, with his mouth full.

"I'm guessing she didn't report it?"

He shook his head, still engrossed in his double quarter pounder with cheese.

"Definitely male?"

"She seemed to think so." He wiped his mouth with the back of his hand. "It was someone with a hood pulled up over their head. That was all she said."

"Mmm, like on the science building CCTV."

"Oh, yeah, that's a point."

Kelly rolled her eyes again. "Come on Jack, follow the plot." She watched him take another big, sloppy bite. "Yuck, I can't look at this any longer. I'm going for a coffee. After you've finished pushing that into your face, you can do another background check on Juliet Bailey. The first one didn't turn up much, so have a good dig around, will you?"

He gave her a thumbs up.

It was late. Everyone had gone home, but Kelly still sat at her desk, aimlessly surfing the Web. She had been hungry a little while ago, but the look and smell of Robson's burger had made her feel sick, and she had now gone past it. She found herself in an aimless frame of mind, too tired to do anything very constructive but unwilling to stop trying.

I can't get interested in Alec Whickham's sexual preferences, quite frankly. She was still sure that Thackray had something to do with Alec's death, but she didn't know what. She flipped back through her and Robson's notes of their meeting with him, but nothing really stood out. *OK, so, he's a creationist, but there's no law against that. He lives in a weird house with a weird name but, again, so do lots of people. What else was he interested in? Oh yes, that Occam's razor thing. What exactly is that all about then?* With an underlying feeling that she was clutching at straws, she hit Wikipedia and searched for William of Ockham. What she found made her jaw drop.

'Although he is commonly known for Occam's razor, the methodological principle that bears his name, William of Ockham also produced significant works on logic, physics, and theology. In the Church of England his day of commemoration is 10 April.'

18

Kelly got into work early the following day. Robson came in half an hour after her, wet through from being caught in a sharp shower walking from the car park. "Honestly, it would bloody wait until I get out of the car!"

"Get your coat off, sit down and listen to this," replied Kelly, demonstrating no sympathy.

"Thanks boss." He took his coat off and shook it, showering water in the immediate vicinity.

"For God's sake, Jack!"

"Sorry ma'am, didn't know it would spread that far," he said, but his grin showed otherwise when he turned his back on her to hang up his coat.

"What was the date Alec Whickham was killed?" asked Kelly, as he sat down at his desk.

"Tenth of April. Why?"

"Because that just happens to be the annual C of E commemoration day for William of Ockham, Thackray's hero."

He didn't react. "So what?"

"Yeah, OK, I know. I can't put it all together yet either." Kelly felt her earlier excitement beginning to fade. *Maybe it was just a coincidence.* "Did the latest check on Bailey bring up anything new?"

"I asked Lyn Parkinson to do it yesterday. I'll see if she turned anything up." Robson stood up again and walked over to the desk of a young female officer on the other side of the room. Kelly drummed her fingers on the desk in impatience. *What the hell is going on in this case. And how are all these people connected?*

She heard Robson's exclamation clear across the office. "Shit!"

He almost ran back to her desk. "It's Bailey. Her maiden name was only Thackray!"

Kelly got up and took her jacket off the back of her chair. "How the hell did we miss that the first time round?" Robson opened his mouth to reply but she cut him short and hurried out of the room. "Never mind, let's go!"

"To Bailey's house?" Robson asked, retrieving his wet raincoat from the coat stand and running after her.

"Oh, we have a lot to talk to Doctor Luke Thackray about first, I think," replied Kelly.

"Do we?" He trotted down the corridor after her. "We don't even know if they are actually related." She broke into a canter in front of him and he had to run to keep up. "Ma'am, exactly what are we going to ask him?"

To: e.mountford@pg.unwe.ac.uk
From: m.osewe@unwe.ac.uk
Re: PhD research supervision
24th April   08:15
Egraine,

Following our meeting yesterday I'm afraid that I'm not in a position to supervise your research due to personal commitments. I'm sure you'll be able to find someone in the faculty who is better qualified to help you.

Regards

Mike Osewe

To: m.osewe@unwe.ac.uk
From: e.mountford@pg.unwe.ac.uk
Re: PhD research supervision
24th April   11:08
Dr Osewe,

I'm sorry you feel that we couldn't work together in a way that might stimulate both of us, but I understand your decision. This morning I have contacted Dr Raman Sharples to see if he might be willing to step in. Reflecting on our meeting yesterday, I, too, feel that working with you on my PhD would be unlikely to satisfy my needs.

Egraine.

Mike read Egraine's email with a sense of relief. The sideswipe about satisfying her wasn't lost on him, but he really didn't care. If she thought that saying Raman might step into his shoes would make him jealous, she couldn't be further away from the truth. He just wanted to forget about yesterday. The evening had been a nightmare; trying to hide his guilt and remorse from Sophie had been so difficult, but he made out he was feeling ill and needed an early night. This morning he had woken up with a clearer head and now, after this email exchange, it seemed that he would be able to free himself from Egraine. The tone of her reply made it apparent she understood that there would be nothing more between them. If she complained to the university it could wreck his relationship and his career, but it didn't sound like she would react to his rejection that way. At least, he hoped not.

19

They stood in front of the wall again, feeling like a raiding party from a medieval siege. Kelly turned to Robson. "Well, you'd better ring the bell." He pressed the button in the centre of the metal rose; the turquoise of its heavy patina was the only colour that broke up the otherwise dull red of the brickwork. They heard the front door of the house open and, through the wrought iron gate, saw Luke Thackray walking down the steps to the front wall.

"Here we go," whispered Robson.

The bolt was drawn from behind the wooden gate and Thackray peered round it. "Yes?"

Kelly was impatient, and it showed. "Could we come in, please? We need to talk to you."

He moved back as she pushed the gate and stepped through the gateway, followed closely by Robson. Wordlessly, Thackray turned and motioned them up the garden path to the front door of the house then closed and re-barred the gate. They carried on through the front door and back to the parlour they had been in on their visit the previous week. They sat down as Thackray followed them in. He stood by the empty fireplace.

"What can I do for you?" he asked.

Kelly leaned forward with her elbows on her knees. "Some further information has come to light regarding Alec Whickham's death. I'll come straight to the point. Are you related to a Professor Juliet Bailey?"

He looked somewhat taken aback. "Well, yes. But what's that got to do with anything?"

"What's the nature of your relationship? And why didn't you tell us the last time we interviewed you?"

"Juliet is my niece. I knew you'd arrested her on suspicion of being involved in Whickham's death, but that's completely ludicrous and I'm sure you'll find that she had nothing to do with it. She hasn't actually been charged, has she?"

Kelly shook her head.

Thackray looked vaguely amused. "Exactly. Actually, I see very little of Juliet. We have ..." He paused. "... very different views of the world. So, I repeat, I didn't know Alec Whickham. I never met him." He looked increasingly in control as he leaned on the mantelpiece.

"You have to admit that there's an increasing number of coincidences," answered Kelly, now feeling less confident and beginning to flounder. "First we have the coincidence of your ID being logged onto one of the computers in the lab from where the blog comments were sent. Now the coincidence of Juliet Bailey being your niece, and her card was used to access the lab where Alec Whickham died."

Thackray remained unruffled. "I cannot explain the first, and the second is of no relevance. It is, as you say, a coincidence."

Kelly didn't know how to reply. She was sure that between Bailey and Thackray there was some important connection to Alec Whickham's murder. But now she was beginning to feel that she was on a badly thought-out fishing trip and, worse, that Thackray knew it. Oh God, I should have stopped to think for longer before rushing here. I need to get my thoughts back into some kind of order. What is it about this man that makes me lose my cool?

Robson came to the rescue. "You're Professor Bailey's Uncle? You don't look much older than her." God bless you Jack, thought Kelly.

Thackray was quiet for a moment, looking as if he were trying to make up his mind about something. He appeared to decide. "Excuse me a minute while I just go and get something." He left the room and walked down the hallway. They heard him climb the stairs and walk into the room directly above them.

"What's all this about, do you think?" asked Robson.

"I've no idea," replied Kelly, with a heavy sigh. "Oh," she smiled, "and thanks, Jack."

He smiled back with feigned surprise. "What for?"

Enough said.

They heard Thackray walk back across the floor and down the stairs. He appeared in the lounge doorway carrying an ornately carved wooden box about eighteen inches square and twelve inches deep. He set it down on the coffee table between himself and the two police officers and sat back in the armchair again.

"What's this?" asked Kelly, with a slight hint of irritation in her voice. She'd come here to get evidence that would help to nail Alec Whickham's murder on Thackray and she wasn't doing a very good job of it. It made her unkindly disposed to any distractions.

He put his hands on the lid of the box, palms down. "This is the Thackray family history. Well, more correctly, what I've been able to find of it." He slid his hands around the edges of the lid and opened it, revealing sets of neatly tied papers, documents and envelopes. "I've always had an interest in genealogy, and my family seems to have had more than its fair share of hoarders. So, I've been able to piece together quite a bit of our family tree. Here it is." He took a couple of papers from the top of the box and handed them to Kelly and Robson. Each showed the same copy of a branched diagram.

"As you can see, there is only nine years between Juliet and myself. She is the eldest child of my eldest brother, Matthew."

"Ah, yes," said Kelly. She scanned back up the tree. "You certainly go in for large families."

A strange look passed over Thackray's face; a mix of pleasure and apprehension. "Does anything else strike you?" he asked.

They both looked back at the diagram, but Kelly was still too agitated to concentrate on it. "I really don't have the time to play games, Doctor Thackray. If there's something important here, just say it."

Robson leaned forward. "What sex was the first child of Juliet and Jeremiah? The one that died at three days old?"

Kelly looked at him in astonishment. "What?"

Thackray's eyes lit up and he sat on the edge of his chair. "Ah, yes, you've seen it Sergeant. That's exactly the question. Jeremiah was English, but Juliet was from America and they married there. They came to settle in England about a year later, but no one even knew about the existence of the lost child until I found this letter." He pulled out a pack of envelopes, tied with a red ribbon. He took one of the envelopes out of the pack, extracted a letter and handed it to Robson. "Let alone its sex."

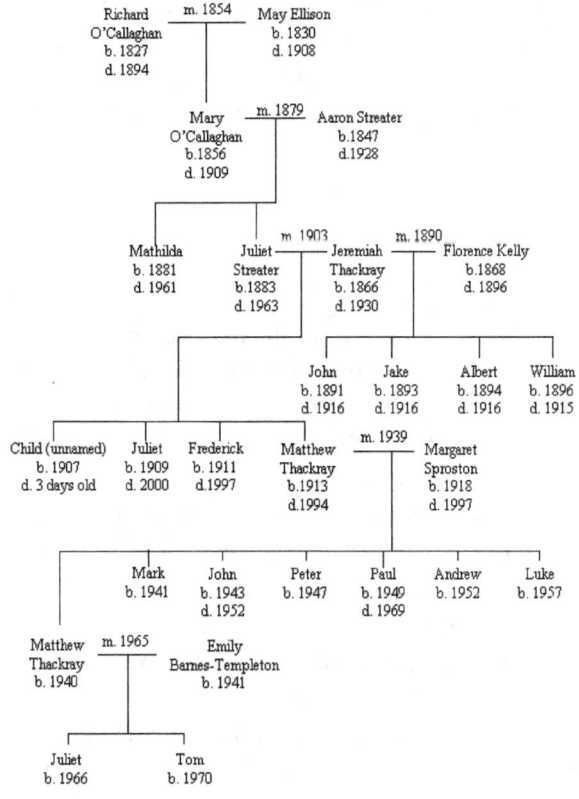

Extract from the Thackray family tree

Despite herself, Kelly was becoming intrigued; she read the letter over his shoulder.

"Ah, right," said Robson. "So you are, then."

Thackray nodded and fluffed up with pride.
This was a new experience for Kelly. Usually she was
way ahead of Jack Robson and waiting for him to
catch up. Now she began to understand how he felt,
and it wasn't nice. *Why can't I see anything? Am I
getting too carried away with my zeal for pinning
Whickham's murder on Thackray?* There was certainly
something about the man that engendered a feeling
of dislike in her.

"OK, can someone please tell me what's going
on?" asked Kelly in exasperation.

Thackray looked at Kelly with a mixture of
disdain and condescension. "I am the seventh son of
a seventh son. Magickal. With a 'k'. Truly mystical.
Not the stuff of cheap tricks."

Kelly looked back at the family tree with a
sinking feeling. "Ah, I see." *Damn him! He's mad. I'll
never get anything to stick to him now.*

Thackray looked across at Robson as though Kelly were no longer there. "You know what is written about seventh sons, Sergeant?"

Robson looked a little awkward. "I just know about Johnny Thunder," he mumbled.

Thackray and Kelly both looked baffled. "Who?" asked Kelly.

"A DC Comics hero in the 1940s. He was one of the Justice Society. You know, superheroes saving the world. Anyway, he was the seventh son of a seventh son and so he had special powers." He saw the looks on their faces. "What? I'm interested in comic heroes. Lots of people are."

"Mmm, getting back to Alec Whickham." said Kelly. She turned to Thackray. "He was killed on the tenth of April. Considering your veneration of William of Ockham, you can understand why we might be curious about it."

His reaction was difficult to read, although he seemed surprised that Kelly would know about Ockham's commemoration day. "Another coincidence. As I told you at our last meeting, I was at the parish council meeting until nine pm that day. Then I came home." He bit his bottom lip and looked uneasy.

Finally, I'm getting somewhere. "And you didn't go out again after that?"

"Not afterwards, no."

Robson picked up on the ambiguity of his answer. "What about before the meeting?"

Thackray took a deep breath and looked at the picture on the wall above the dresser. "Every year I make a small offering to William on his day. Something appropriate. A razor. I lay it in the sea so that it will not be disturbed by the hand of man. This year I went down to the shore to make the offering before going on to the parish council. But if you're suggesting that I would take a human life as a sacrifice, that is sickening and outrageous. I would never take a life, Inspector. Never. And I certainly do not believe it would honour William to do so."

His sincerity was clear, and Kelly began to feel her certainty slipping away. She folded her copy of the Thackray family tree and put it in her bag. "Thank you, Doctor Thackray. I think we've got as far as we can for now. You won't mind if I keep the family tree?"

"Not at all," said Thackray, the little flame of pride beginning to rekindle in his eyes.

Kelly got up and Robson followed. Thackray led them down the garden path again and bolted the wooden door behind them, with a curt "Goodbye."

They got into the car and Kelly put her head in her hands. "Oh God! What a total disaster. That was not the high spot of my career. What the hell is wrong with me?"

"Don't be too hard on yourself, ma'am. He's a slippery fish, and barking mad," said Robson, mixing his metaphors. "What powers does he think he's got?"

"God knows. I certainly don't anymore."

"Where to now?"

"Somewhere where I can think. Would you drop me off at the North Beach? I'll walk back."

20

Robson pulled into the lay by and Kelly got out. She leaned back into the car. "I may wander around for a while. When you get back to the office have a ferret around for ... something. Anything. Just take a flyer. We're completely missing something, and I don't know what it is." He nodded. "And thanks again, Jack." She shut the door.

He drove away, smiling to himself. How many times had he done this when they were on a case? *She's a good copper. Just thinks too much.*

Kelly bought a large ice cream cone from the kiosk at the top of the slipway and then walked down onto the flat expanse of sand. She could hardly see the sea. At this time of year, just after a new or full moon, the sea can go out a long way; even further than usual, which is saying something for this coastline. But twice a day it races back across the sand flats towards the sea wall. The speed of the tides and the treacherous areas of quicksand claim lives on this coast every year, but it was hard to believe it on a day like this. The sky was deep azure directly above her head, fading to pale turquoise at the horizon. The few clouds were high and thin, like the flanks of colossal fish, their scales shimmering in the sunlight. The distant sea twinkled. She sat down at the bottom of the slipway and took her shoes and socks off with one hand, carefully holding onto the ice cream cone with the other. She rolled up her black trousers and set off across the sand, keeping parallel with the sea front and Marine Drive.

OK. Let's think this through from the start. Bailey's ID card was used to open the lab door the night Whickham was killed. She would know that her card would be traceable, so why would she use it? Why would anyone use it? She could have lent it to Thackray, but it's still too incriminating. No, the obvious answer is that someone did it to frame her, or at least put us off the scent. Putting absorbent paper soaked with Whickham's blood into her own dustbin was another stupid thing to do, and it seems out of character for her. Again, it looks like too much incriminating evidence. Amateur. So, is that what the blog postings are about too? Is it someone who knows her relationship to Luke Thackray and is trying to put both of them in the frame? So how did they get hold of Thackray's ID? Shit. None of this makes sense. She took a big bite out of the chocolate flake that was speared into the top of her ice cream. *But Thackray still makes my nose twitch.*

When she had finished the ice cream she took her iPod out of her bag and chose her favourite album for walking and thinking; R.E.M.'s 'Automatic for the People'. The shuffle started at 'Star Me Kitten' as she walked along the sand, lost in the music, her thoughts and the beauty of her surroundings. About ten minutes later she reached a set of steps and realised that she was near the bottom of University Road. She thought about calling in to see Joseph, just on the off chance of a helpful chat, and then noticed that her heart was beating a little faster at the thought. She pulled her socks and shoes back on and rolled down her trouser legs, brushing off the sand that had gathered in the turn ups. With a lighter step she headed towards the UNWE science building, despite R.E.M.'s warning that everybody hurts, sometimes.

The receptionist pointed Kelly in the direction of Mike and Joseph's office. As she walked down the corridor she felt a flutter in her stomach. *Oh, stop this.*

She found the door and knocked. "Come in." *Was that Joseph's voice?* She checked the room number again. *S119. That's what the man at the desk said.* She opened the door and looked in. Mike and Joseph were at their desks and both looked up.

"Oh, Inspector Kelly. Hello." Joseph got up and walked over to her with his hand out. They shook hands and he turned round towards Mike. "You've met Doctor Mike Osewe?"

Mike stood up. "Yes, you interviewed me the day Alec died."

"Indeed. Hello again." They shook hands.

Joseph pulled a spare chair up to the side of his desk. "Please, have a seat. Did we have an appointment I've forgotten?"

"Oh, no. I was just passing." She cringed inwardly. *You idiot. You could think of something more convincing than that.* "Sorry, dreadful cliché." Mike and Joseph both grinned. "It would help me if I could run some things past you."

"Sure. We'll help however we can," said Joseph, as Mike nodded in agreement and brought his chair round to Joseph's desk.

Kelly took a deep breath. "We've been investigating a divinity lecturer here, a Doctor Luke Thackray."

"Is he the blogger?" asked Mike, quick as a flash.

"I didn't say that," said Kelly. "But you may choose to draw that conclusion. Anyway, he's quite a character." She opened her bag, took out the

Thackray family tree and held it so they could both see. "A seventh son of a seventh son. He believes he's magickal. With a 'k'."

Mike and Joseph both laughed. "Is he loopy enough to write the stuff on Alec's blog?" asked Mike.

"Very probably, but he swears he didn't."

Joseph had been looking at the family tree closely. "Actually, he's the seventh son of a sixth son, according to this."

"Ah, well, Juliet and Jeremiah's baby who died was male. Thackray found a letter from Juliet's sister in America in the early 1900s confirming the death and the child's sex."

"So he counts that does he?"

"Apparently."

It was Mike's turn to study the tree. "May Ellison," he said, under his breath.

Kelly half heard it. "Pardon?"

"Oh, er, did you say Juliet Streater was from America?"

"Yes, somewhere in the South I think. Hang on." She consulted her notebook. "Yes. Sumterville, South Carolina."

Mike raised his eyebrows.

Joseph turned to Kelly. "Juliet seems to be quite a popular name in that family." He looked at her quizzically.

"Yes, it does, doesn't it." Kelly dropped her voice to just above a whisper. "You both know Juliet Bailey well, don't you?"

"I know her fairly well," Joseph replied.

"Do you know anything about her family, or how any of this Thackray business might be connected? I just can't piece all this together."

"No. She never says anything much about her family. I know she divorced a few years ago and has no children. Her parents live in the Midlands somewhere and her dad is a retired archaeology professor. That's it, that's all I know." He looked back at the family tree. "So Luke Thackray is her ..." He paused to work it out. "...uncle?"

Kelly nodded. "How well do you know Professor Bailey, Doctor Osewe?"

"Hardly at all, I'm afraid. At least, not personally. I know her work and, of course, she's the Dean so we talk sometimes. But only about work." He gently took the copy of the Thackray family tree from Kelly's hand and looked at it. "It is an odd coincidence that her card was used to open the lab door, and that she's related to someone who may be the phantom blogger, though."

"Coincidences seem to be all we have at the moment," Kelly replied.

"Could I take a quick photocopy of this?" asked Mike, standing up.

"Sure. Thackray seems to be very happy to hand out copies."

He walked over to the printer, put the paper on the glass and closed the lid. A bright white light flashed back and forth around the edges of the cover.

Joseph shrugged. "Well, I'm sorry we can't shed any more light on things. But I'm going over to see Juliet this evening, just for a supportive chat. I could do some careful rummaging, if you'd like?"

Kelly looked uncertain. "Very careful. I shouldn't really be involving you both in this at all, but any extra background information you can give me would be very helpful just at the moment. Today hasn't been my best day for making good judgements. Please don't make it worse by getting yourselves into difficult positions." She got up and took the Thackray family tree back from Mike's outstretched hand. "I'd better be making my way back to the station. I walked over."

"I can give you a lift back, if you'd like?" asked Joseph.

"No, really. It's not that far and walking helps me to think. Thanks, though." She smiled at them both as she walked out of the room. "Bye."

She walked back towards the beach. 'Drive,' sang Michael Stipe.

Robson sat in front of his computer, staring blankly at the screen. The boss had said he should have a ferret around. *For what, exactly?* He looked back at his notebook, hoping for inspiration. He spotted 'weird house ... weird name', but he hadn't written the name down. And he hadn't taken any notice this morning, either.

Bugger! What was it again? Albion? No, something like that though. Pan something. Panalbion? He tried this in the Google search bar and hit the button. Lots of hits for companies called Pan Albion, but nothing that looked like it would be helpful. *It wasn't Panalbion, anyway. It was ... was ... panoglion? Panolbion? That was it!* He tried it in the search bar. It came up with 'Panolbion, or the blessedness of the saints, by AS, Preacher of the Word' ...

Now, that does look interesting. It had been published in England in 1634 and attributed to two likely authors, Archibald Symmer or Aaron Streater. On an impulse he picked up the transcripts of the blog comments that Joseph had given them and put a few phrases of the later, more religious allusions in his search toolbar. Nothing. *OK, one last try.* He went back to the search results for Panolbion and looked to see if there were any full transcripts available. There was one in the Australian government library, of all places. He hit the link, hoping that he'd be able to download it. *Yes!* A pdf version was available for download. It was a short pamphlet of dense and difficult text; largely what would now be considered ramblings about the way to ensure a place in heaven. *So, a Carolingian religious diatribe.* He smiled to himself. *I bet she'd never guess I knew words like that.* He copied and pasted the text into a Word document and then chose two of the phrases from the blog comments that looked like quotes:

'God who knows the heart, accepteth the affect for the effect, and the will for the deed.'
'None can learn the art of dying well, without the life of righteousness.'

That second one was particularly disturbing. He ran a search in the Word document and gasped when it found the exact match.

Maybe she was right about Thackray all along.

21

Joseph sat in Juliet's lounge, watching a deep red sunset bleed through the budding branches of the oak tree at the side of her garden. The cherry trees were in full bloom at the far end of the lawn, and through them he could just make out the Rufus Court postgraduate residences. He heard her bustling about in the kitchen, making a pot of tea.

Joseph was becoming increasingly concerned about Juliet. She had been at home on paid leave since Alec's death with little contact from the university; the senior managers seemed to want to distance themselves until her guilt or innocence had been decided upon. As long as she had work to do he thought she would probably be able to lose herself in it. But she was reaching the end of the paper she was writing and lack of access to the university, and all the networks she relied upon, must be a looming dread for her. He'd been to see her the previous week, and although she had put a brave face on it he had seen that her edges were beginning to fray. And now it was a week later with no further progress in the police investigation, and he had to try to find out about a mad, magickal uncle. With a 'k'. *How am I even going to start this conversation?*

Juliet came into the room carrying a tray. She put it down on the table between them. It was neatly laid out with a white porcelain teapot, a cream jug and sugar bowl. The cups and saucers were in matching Wedgewood. A small stainless steel tea strainer sat in its drip cup. Juliet still clung to the tradition of making leaf tea, which she got by post from a specialist supplier every month. Tippy

Golden Flowery Orange Pekoe from Assam; deeply aromatic with a perfect astringency.

"So, how are you?" asked Joseph as he leaned over to pour the tea.

"No, not yet!" she snapped.

He looked startled and put the teapot back down on the tray. "Sorry."

"Oh no, Joseph, I'm the one who's sorry." She smiled at him weakly. "I overreact to everything at the moment. The tea will just take another minute or two to brew."

He smiled. "Don't worry, I understand. Have you heard from anyone else at the university yet?" he asked, as he leaned back in the chair.

She shook her head. "No, just you." She leaned over and touched him on the arm. "For which I'm very grateful." She sat back. "I think the VC is just keeping his head down until the police have finished their enquiries."

"What about friends and family?"

"My mother and father came last weekend. It was lovely to see them and a huge support. Oh, and Jim called."

"Jim? Your ex-husband?" asked Joseph.

"The very same! It was kind of him, actually. He did offer to come up and see me, but I put him off. At least for now. "

"Do you stay in touch with him?"

"Only occasionally," Juliet replied. "There's no real animosity between us. But we have very little in common. We never did have many similar interests, to be honest. I think that's partly where it went wrong."

She seemed to want to open up, so Joseph pursued it. Perhaps he could get her to talk about her wider family, too. "I remember Jim used to work at The Royal, but where is he now?"

"Oh, he's part of a private practice in London. More lucrative than the NHS, and more up his street, really."

Keep her talking. "I only met him a couple of times, but he seemed like a quiet chap."

Juliet nodded. "It may seem a strange thing to say under the present circumstances, but I suppose I recognised some of my ex-husband's characteristics in Alec, if I'm honest."

"Surely not!" laughed Joseph.

"Towards the end of my marriage it was more pleasant to be in work than at home. People were caring and interested and responsive at work. I came home and it was ... I was ..." She stared out of the window and seemed to drift away.

"Juliet? Are you O.K?"

"Sorry, what was I saying?" She picked up the teapot and swirled it. "Oh yes. No one likes coming second repeatedly in a relationship. Jim seemed to owe greater commitments to anyone other than me. His job, his family, his social clubs. All the occasions when he let his attention be demanded by someone else were logical and sounded reasonable in their own right. But when you put them all together the compound effect simply left me with a sense of being unimportant to him."

Joseph nodded towards the swirling teapot. "Is that tea ready yet?"

Juliet smiled at him. "Of course." She placed the tea strainer over one of the cups, poured in the golden brown liquid and passed it over the table to him.

"You've always come across as being very devoted to your career," said Joseph, pouring milk into his cup. "Maybe he felt that was threatening?"

"He didn't feel anything very strongly I don't think. Except impatience. And anger if he didn't get his own way on something he really wanted. But you're right. Living with me wasn't always a picnic for Jim either. And in a way I guess my career is partly down to him. I threw myself into my work initially to fill the gaps when I'd get home and he wasn't there. When I started to get some successes and recognition, I found it a really important part of my life."

"How long were you together?" Joseph asked.

"Fifteen years. It's a long time, but the effect of drifting apart is slow. A gradual degradation. And I always felt that it would be harder to leave than to stay. But eventually that began to change."

"It still must have been a wrench though, to make the break."

Juliet shook her head. "Not really. I guess my overwhelming feeling in my marriage to Jim was loneliness. I even felt lonely when we were together. Most of the time he wasn't there mentally. He was off in his own world and I could make a comment about something, a joke or whatever, and get no response. He talked to himself much more than he ever talked to me. I had been alone in so many ways for so much of the time that when the break came it wasn't as traumatic for me as I had feared. Ironically Jim had a much harder time of it. He'd been used to living with the sense of me being there. For years I'd been living with the sense of him not being there. But there was no acrimony when we split. I'd thrown myself into my work so much by then that I didn't feel any real remorse, just relief. And my family were very supportive"

This is my chance. "Do you have family around here?"

"Well, yes, but my parents live in Telford. There are uncles and cousins still living near here, but I rarely see them. I don't have much to do with my father's side of the family."

"Any particular reason?" asked Joseph. Juliet's eyes narrowed, just slightly. He rushed to explain. "I don't mean to pry. It seems to be helping you to talk. I didn't mean to be nosey." *For God's sake, try not to interrogate her! I'm really no good at this.*

She smiled and relaxed. "You're right. It is therapeutic. And you're being very patient to listen to all this." She giggled. "Between you and me, my father's side of the family is a little ... eccentric. Nothing serious. Just a bit ..." She whirled her finger around her ear.

"Oh dear." Joseph smiled and took a long, slow sip of his tea, leaving a space in the conversation for Juliet to fill. But she didn't seem inclined to. *Now what do I do?* He put his cup down and leant forward in a confidential manner. "To tell you the truth, one of my uncles is a bit odd. Thinks he can do real magic or something, poor soul." He watched her closely. Her body sagged as a heavy weight suddenly seemed to descend on her.

"Well, it's going to take more than imaginary magical powers to retrieve my career. Whatever the final outcome of all this, it's all over, isn't it? Guilty or innocent." Her head bowed. "We've both spent enough time in the field to know that mud sticks."

"No, Juliet. I don't believe that, and neither should you. Try to stay positive."

She looked straight at him and he saw the depth of the distress in her eyes. "I do try, but when I get tired, it's hard. Sorry Joseph, but I think I need to get some rest."

He stood up. "Sure. Of course." He gave her a hug and let himself out. *Well,* he thought, *could I have been any less subtle? But, she did seem to be affected by talking about her family, so maybe there is something in the Luke Thackray connection.* He made a mental note to call Kelly in the morning.

Sophie had gone to bed early, tired and feeling sick, so Mike sat at the computer in the study and logged on for one last look at his emails.

To: Rifleclub
From: garym@student.unwe.ac.uk
Re: club night next week
Date: 24th April   18:46
Hi All,

I've got my hands on a Winchester Model 1876! A present from my dad. I'm bringing it to the club open shoot next Sunday, so come along and have a go. I've made up some loads with black powder!! Mike O, it would be really good if you could make it cos I know old guns are your thing and I'd like to ask you a couple things about it. Be there man!

Gary

Reply to: garym@student.unwe.ac.uk
From: m.osewe@unwe.ac.uk
Re: club night next week
Date: 24th April   22:10
Hi Gary,
Sure will.
Mike

Mike had a lifelong interest in guns, particularly antique ones. Being brought up in Africa and England, of both African and English parentage, he had heard the stories of British explorers in Africa and had especially been fascinated by the story of Stanley and Livingstone. When three of Sir Henry Morton Stanley's guns came up for auction at Holt's in September 2009, Mike had scraped together £10,000 from savings and a loan and gone along to the auction. The gun he really wanted was the Winchester .45-75 Model 1876 lever action rifle; the guide price was £7,000 - £9,000. But that was never a realistic estimate. The gun had attracted many stories, most of them likely to be apocryphal, that attributed it as the firearm that single-handedly saved Stanley's Congo and Emin Pasha expeditions. At the auction Mike was rapidly outbid, with the gun eventually selling for £35,000. But Winchester rifles had remained a particular interest, so now that one of his rifle club colleagues had given him the opportunity to shoot one, he couldn't resist. Particularly the 1876 model. He was really looking forward to it.

22

It was Robson's turn to get into work early this time. Kelly was intrigued when she walked into the office and saw him already sitting behind his desk, his head buried in papers. She took off her jacket and draped it over the back of her chair, then stood and waited for him to look up at her. He didn't.

"Insomnia?" she prompted.

He jumped. "Oh hi. No." Then he grinned. "Enlightenment."

She sat down. "Go on then, enlighten me."

"It's about Thackray," he said. Kelly's eyes widened. "I thought that would interest you. You remember the name of his house?"

"Oh, something odd. I can't bring it to mind," she said. "What's that got to do with anything?"

"The name is Panolbion. It turns out that Panolbion is the name of a religious text, written by someone with the initials A.S. in 1634. I managed to download a copy last night and ran a search for any of the entries on Alec Whickham's blog. Take a look." He handed over a stapled copy of Panolbion and a couple of sheets of paper with the blog comments. The corresponding text was highlighted with a bright yellow pen.

Kelly looked at the papers with a widening smile. "Well, well, well. It doesn't prove anything but it's one more coincidence to add to the list, eh?"

"There's another one too. The author of Panolbion is 'A.S. Preacher of the Word', and the general consensus is that it was either an Archibold Symmer or Aaron Streater. Either of those ring a bell?"

Kelly wrinkled her brow. "No. Should they?"

Robson passed another piece of paper over to her. It was Thackray's family tree. "Who married Mary O'Callaghan?"

"Good God. Aaron Streater. But it can't be the same one. There's almost two hundred years between them."

"I'm guessing Aaron is a family name, and that the house name Panolbion has probably been passed down too. Whatever the explanation, it's a really obscure reference for someone to try to frame Thackray with." He paused. "You know, I think Thackray did write those blog comments."

Kelly had just opened her mouth to agree when her mobile rang. She looked at who was calling. Joseph Connor. She felt a little heart skip as she took the call, but didn't forget to mouth "well done Jack" across at Robson.

"Doctor Connor. How are you?"

"Good thanks. I thought I'd just fill you in on my visit with Juliet last night."

"Oh, yes. I hope it wasn't difficult for you?"

Joseph laughed. "No, not really. But I'm a bloody hopeless interrogator!"

Kelly smiled. "Did anything come up?"

"Well, she did say she had uncles who still live locally, but she didn't mention Luke Thackray specifically. She said she didn't see much of them and that one of them was somewhat eccentric, so I put my big foot in my mouth and said I had a mad uncle who thought he could do magic. Just to try to draw her out."

"And did it?"

"No. The exact opposite, actually. She clammed up and said she was tired, so I left."

"Well, that sounds like a kind of result."

Joseph sighed. "Yeah, it did seem to affect her, but I still don't know if we were talking about her uncle Luke or one of the others."

"Don't worry Doctor Connor. That's useful information for us anyway. It was a long shot. In any case, other things have come up that may cast some more light on this, so please don't try to take it any further."

"What things?"

"Hmm, I can't tell you that. But thanks for the information, and I'll be in touch. Bye."

"Bye."

She closed the call and looked across at Robson. "Connor saw Bailey last night and had a bit of a chat about her family, it seems. Anyway, she admits to having a mad uncle but that's about all."

Robson nodded. "So, do we pay Doctor Thackray another visit?"

Kelly thought for a moment. "I think we need to take it more carefully this time. I barged in last time without thinking. The picture is still fuzzy, so perhaps we need to go and see Juliet Bailey and do some more probing. Let's have a think about it today and go and see her on Monday." She smiled at Robson. "That was a really good job on the Panolbion link, Jack. We'll make a detective of you yet!"

23

It was Saturday afternoon. Mike and Sophie had been out shopping in the morning, but it had worn Sophie out and she was snoozing with her feet up on the sofa. Mike went up to his study and unfolded the photocopy of the Thackray family tree. It was that name, May Ellison, and the Sumterville connection that fascinated him. He had an interest in slave history and recognised Ellison as the name of a freed slave in South Carolina, who went on to be a successful plantation owner. It seemed like quite a coincidence that someone with that name should be in the Sumterville area, so he set about doing a bit of research.

It wasn't difficult. Within a couple of hours, internet searches had enabled him to unearth a lot of information on William Ellison Jnr. Born in 1790, he had started life with the name April. A strange name for a boy, but it was a popular practice to name slave children after the month of their birth. Around the age of twelve, April was owned by a white slave-owner named William Ellison, son of a Robert Ellison of Fairfield County, South Carolina. Although Mike couldn't find any hard evidence to say who April's father was, the general consensus seemed to be that either Robert or William had fathered the child with one of the family's female slaves. In some documents he was described as "yellow" rather than black; a reference to being of mixed race parentage. Certainly, he was picked out for special treatment by the family. He trained as a cotton gin machinist and learned to read, write and keep accounts. By 1816 he had earned enough money to buy his freedom, and that of his wife and daughter. He moved to Sumterville and opened up a cotton gin repair business. In 1820 he bought his first two slaves and applied for his name to be changed to William Ellison Jnr, in recognition of his good treatment by his former master, or possibly in recognition of his biological father. In either case, his business and his family went from strength to strength. In 1850 he owned three hundred and eighty six acres of land and thirty seven slaves and by 1860 he was South Carolina's largest slave owner. By then only five percent of the population of South Carolina owned as much real estate as William Ellison Jnr. His wealth was fifteen times greater than that of the state's average for those of European descent and he was in the top one percent of slave owners in the whole of the South. *Wow,* thought Mike. *Is this an extreme form of Stockholm Syndrome or what!*

Apparently, Ellison was not renowned for being particularly supportive of his slaves and he didn't free a single one in all his working life. Although he looked after their health well, he had a pretty hard reputation otherwise. He died in December 1861 and his will left everything to his family. Except for a five hundred dollar bequest to May Ellison, a female slave child he had sold in 1838. Hmm, interesting and somewhat out of character. William wasn't the kind of man to leave money to his slaves for no reason. She must have been very special, despite the fact that he had sold her, as he did most of his female slave children. *Probably his illegitimate daughter, then. So, the Thackrays are partly descended from African American slaves! You wouldn't think it to look at them now, but that's four to five generations later, so plenty of opportunity for gene dilution.* He looked at the Thackray family tree again. May married someone called Richard O'Callaghan. *Sounds Irish. I wonder who he was?*

Mike stood up and walked to the bathroom. He looked at himself in the mirror and wondered how his and Sophie's child might look. He really hadn't thought about it before now. Sophie had blonde hair and pale skin; a typical blue-eyed northern European. If the next couple of generations of his descendants married people of similar European racial background, would his mother's heritage be noticeable in Mike's future descendants at all? He was roused from his thoughts by Sophie coming into the bathroom. She gave him a hug from behind, standing on her toes and resting her chin on his shoulder.

"Yes, you're absolutely gorgeous!"

He laughed and turned to her, gently patting her slightly swollen belly. "I'm just wondering what junior will look like. A bit of both of us, I expect."

She stroked his cheek. "Well, if he or she has your looks, they'll get by just fine. Now, I desperately need to pee so clear off!"

"OK. Fancy anything for tea?"

She shuffled him out of the bathroom and closed the door behind him. "Yuck, not really. Oh, actually, could you do me a couple of slices of cheese on toast?"

"Will do. I've just got a quick email to send and then I'll get onto it."

Mike walked back to his study and sat down at his computer.

To: j.connor@unwe.ac.uk
From: m.osewe@unwe.ac.uk
Re: Thackray family tree
Date 26th April   17:55
Joe,

Been doing some research on Thackray's family tree and turned up some really interesting stuff that I think you'll find fascinating. I'll tell you all about it on Monday, but suffice it to say that families are complicated things. The Thackrays seem to have African, American and possibly Irish (O'Callaghan – sounds Irish to me) connections.

See you
Mike.

The next day Mike walked onto the outdoor rifle range filled with excited anticipation. The Winchester was his favourite rifle.

"Hey, Mike my man! Here she is!" Gary Mason, a second year student at UNWE, bent down and picked up a cloth rifle case. He pulled the gun out and handed it to Mike. "So, what do you think?" he said, quietly. There was an echo in the way he said it that made Mike's skin crawl, but he couldn't quite locate the source of his unease. He was able to shake it off quickly though, and concentrate on the gun.

That wasn't difficult. It was a superb specimen, as Gary had said; elegant, with a deep brown walnut straight stock and fore-end, characteristic octagonal barrel and the trademark lever action of early repeating rifles. Mike ran his hand over the wood. It was smooth and cool. "Can't wait to shoot it."

"I think you should have the honour of the first shot then," said Gary, taking the gun off him and burrowing into his bag for the ammunition. He loaded a round into the side chamber. Mike went to pick up his ear defenders from the cage, squared up to the target and shouldered the rifle. The balance was perfect. He lined up the front and back sights and slowly pulled the trigger. The gun went off with a satisfying bang and a good hard kickback. He brought it down from his shoulder. "Bloody fantastic!"

A couple of other members were waiting for their turn to shoot, so Mike passed the gun back to Gary. He loaded singles and each of the members took their shots.

"Come on Mike, want to shoot a few repeaters?" Gary loaded five rounds into the chamber. "After all, that's what this gun is really all about."

Mike stepped back up to the firing line and took the gun. He shouldered it once again and took aim. Again the loud bang and hard kick. He drew the lever down and back, took aim and pulled the trigger smoothly. The explosion burst the stock of the gun clean open and shot the bolt back towards the side of his head.

24

Joseph's mobile rang.

"Joseph, oh thank God." It was Sophie.

"Sophie? What's wrong? Are you OK?" The first thing that went through his mind was that something had gone wrong with her pregnancy.

"It's Mike. A gun blew up. He's in hospital." She was barely managing to talk between sobs.

"Sophie, where are you love?"

"At home. They've just rung me. Mike's got the car. I can't get to him."

"I'll be right there. Just wait love, I'll be as quick as I can. Is he at the Royal?"

"Yes. Sorry. I just didn't know who else to ring."

"No problem love. Just wait and try not to worry. OK?"

"Yes." She rang off.

Anna looked at him in alarm. "What's wrong?"

He picked up his jacket and headed for the door. "It sounds like Mike's had an accident with a gun. He's in the Royal. I'll go and get Sophie and take her over there. She hasn't got the car. Anyway, I don't think she's in any fit state to drive."

"Do you want me to come?" asked Anna.

"No love, I'll call you from the hospital and let you know what happened."

He ran out of the door, got into his car and drove round to Mike and Sophie's house as quickly as he could. The roads were thankfully quiet at this time on a Sunday evening. When he got there Sophie had calmed down a little, but her face was tear-stained and drawn. Joseph bundled her into the car and set off for the hospital. "Did they say how he was?" he asked.

"Not really. Just that there had been an accident and he had a head injury and was unconscious. Oh Joseph, I'm so scared! I don't know what I'd do if I lost him." She burst into tears again.

"I know love. Try not to worry too much. We'll soon see how he is."

Ten minutes later he pulled into the hospital car park, stopped the car and held her until her renewed sobbing died down. "Are you really up to this Sophie? Mike will understand if you don't feel able to go in. Particularly just now. In your condition." *Oh I'm an idiot, nobody says that these days.* "Sorry, that's hopelessly old-fashioned but you know what I mean."

"I'll be fine. I have to see him. To see how he is."

Joseph managed to find the right change for the car park and they hurried into the hospital reception. They were directed to the newly built high-tech wing; an incongruous, flat-roofed appendix to the Victorian façade. They checked in with intensive care reception. Thankfully they didn't have long to wait for the doctor to see them. The good news was that the bolt had grazed Mike's head and only caused a hairline fracture of his skull. He had some burns from the explosion, but they were expected to heal without too much scarring. He had regained consciousness quite quickly after the accident, but the doctors were sedating him overnight and keeping him in intensive care in case any complications arose from the head injury. The bad news was that he had lost the pinna of his right ear and may have sustained some damage to his inner ear. They didn't know the extent of that injury yet, but it was very likely that he would have some hearing loss. Sophie could see him for a few minutes but it would be better if she came back the following day. If everything remained stable overnight they would bring him round from the sedation tomorrow morning and move him out of intensive care.

Sophie grasped Joseph's hand. "Come with me. Please."

Mike was lying on a bed with most of his head lost in dressings. Needles and tubes seemed to be everywhere; machines beeped and digital displays flashed. Sophie walked to the bed, took his hand and squeezed it. There was no response and she looked at Joseph with apprehension.

"He's sedated, love. Things always look worse than they are in hospitals. I'm sure he's going to be alright." But it took all his acting ability to sound confident. Mike looked frighteningly vulnerable, and somehow very small. He was a tall and strongly-built man, and the contrast between his usual appearance and now was disconcerting. Sophie began to shake and suddenly looked very pale. Joseph took hold of her and sat her down on a nearby chair. "Mike's in good hands here. Come on, I'll drive you back. Stay with us tonight. There isn't anything else you can do and you need to rest for your own sake, and the baby's. Have you called your parents?"

She shook her head. "I don't think I can face telling them tonight."

"I'll do it when we get home. Come on – let's get you back to Anna. She'll be dying to look after you." He winked, and Sophie smiled for the first time that evening as they walked out of the hospital into the cool spring air.

25

Sophie had fallen into a fitful sleep in the early hours of Monday morning, so they had decided to let her sleep on rather than try to wake her for breakfast. Joseph put on his jacket as Anna cleared away the breakfast things. "Bye love. I hope Sophie's parents get here soon." He turned to leave the house just as their car turned into the drive. They had left early to travel the couple of hours from their home near Carlisle, and looked drawn and worried as they got out of the car.

"Oh, they're here!" he shouted to Anna, and then walked out to the drive.

Sophie's father put out his hand. "Doctor Connor?" Joseph smiled and nodded. "Thank you so much for taking care of Sophie. We're very grateful."

Joseph grasped the sweaty hand. "Not at all. Mike and Sophie are our good friends. It's the very least we could do."

"Sorry, we should introduce ourselves. Doreen and Cliff Sumner."

Doreen Sumner took hold of Joseph's right hand in both of hers. They were cold as ice. "Thank you for calling us last night, and for taking good care of Sophie. How is she?"

"Still sleeping at the moment, I think. We left her to rest..." He was interrupted by one of the upstairs windows opening and Sophie leaning out to wave to her parents.

Doreen let go of his hand and ran over to the house. "Oh darling. How are you?"

"I'm fine mum. It's Mike we should be worrying about."

Doreen curled her top lip and didn't reply. Joseph led them both in and left Anna to manage the meeting while he left for work.

A knock came at Joseph's office door. "Yes, come in,"

Raman Sharples, associate professor of palaeontology, appeared through the doorway. The usual cheery smile was missing from his round face. "God, Joseph, I just heard about Mike. I'm really sorry. Do you know how he is?"

Joseph motioned him to sit down. "I took Sophie to see him in hospital last night, and they had him sedated in intensive care. But if all went well overnight they were going to move him out to a ward this morning. Sophie's parents have come down and they'll all be over at the hospital now, I would think. I haven't heard anything, so I'm hoping that's good. I'll be going over to see how he is this afternoon, if the doctors will let me see him." He paused. "He's lost an ear."

Raman winced.

"I know," said Joseph, "but it could have been a lot worse, to be honest. He's lucky not to be dead."

Raman shook his head. "On top of this terrible business about Alec. And Juliet being under so much suspicion. It's like something from a TV police drama. Hard to believe any of it." He paused for a moment, trying to find the right words to express what he was thinking. "I'm really sorry for all this, Joe. Alec and Mike were your friends. Well, Mike still is, of course! Oh God, the department is beginning to feel jinxed."

"Yes, I know what you mean." Joseph felt he needed to break the tension, so changed the subject. "Anyway, I haven't seen you since before Easter. Did you manage to get a holiday?"

Raman nodded and appeared to relax a little. "Yes, we did thanks. We didn't go away, but we did take the kids out on day trips. We went down to Chester Zoo for one day. They were fascinated by the chimps. They kept asking me why the chimp compound had water around it and I explained it was to keep them in. They kept asking why the chimps didn't swim to get out and I explained that they don't like water and find it difficult to swim. They were really surprised. They couldn't believe that they looked so much like us but they couldn't really swim. And particularly that they don't like it. The kids love swimming." Raman's countenance clouded again. "Alec would have had an explanation for them."

Joseph nodded. "But I'm not sure it would have been the right one."

"You still have your doubts about the full-blown aquatic theories, then?"

"The full-blown theories, yes. But I'm becoming very convinced about water having a crucial role in human evolution. It's odd, but when I spoke to Alec over the last few weeks before he died he seemed to have hardened his position even further on the aquatic ape hypothesis. He was less and less open to arguments from genetics research, that's for sure."

"And that was odd for Alec?" Raman grinned.

Joseph chuckled. "Well, no. But what was odd was a paper he was working on just a couple of weeks before he died. It was more well-balanced than any of the discussions I'd had with him lately, and it didn't seem to quite match up with his style. It looked to me like he wrote it with someone else, but then there was no other attribution on the draft."

Raman shrugged. "Maybe he had a change of heart but didn't want to admit it to anyone personally."

"Mm, maybe so."

The conversation seemed to be running out of steam, but Joseph had the distinct impression that Raman still hadn't really said what he'd come to say. He let the silence continue, hoping Raman would fill it. Eventually he did.

"Erm, speaking of Alec, I've taken on Egraine Mountford, his research student, as PhD supervisor. Mike was going to supervise her, but she said she thought it wasn't going to work out so she asked me instead. She's looking at bipedalism and hand usage in primates, so actually it fits me quite well. But, now I'm a bit disturbed about it too."

"Yes, I remember her seeing Mike about it. What the problem? Is it not progressing well?"

"Oh, no, I'm not disturbed about her research. She's a bright kid and she's doing good work. No, it's more about her."

"How do you mean?"

"Well, bad luck does seem to follow her, doesn't it? Alec's her supervisor and he's murdered, then Mike moves into the frame and he gets his ear blown off. Hope I'm third time lucky," he joked. But didn't laugh. "Between you and me, she's a bit of a flirt I think. She really seemed to be giving me the eye when we met yesterday. Or maybe that's just the wishful thinking of someone heading for their fortieth birthday!" This time he did laugh. "I just wondered if Alec or Mike said anything about her?"

"No, nothing," answered Joseph. "She was a bit dolled up when she came to see Mike the other day, but he didn't say anything to me about her after their meeting. I can ask him if you like?"

"Oh no," said Raman, standing up. "Don't bother him. I'm probably just exercising a bit of Hindu superstition. I get it from my mother!" He smiled broadly and looked more like his old self, relieved to get his worries out into the open. "Give Mike my best when you see him, won't you."

"Yes, sure."

After Raman had gone, Joseph put his head in his hands and focussed his eyes on infinity. *Jinxed might be a very appropriate description.*

26

The smell of hospital lunch still hung in the air as Joseph walked into the ward with a large box of chocolates that sported an oversized bow on the lid. Anna had insisted on him not going to see Mike empty-handed, even though he tried to explain that men just don't do showy presents for other men. She'd be asking him to buy candles next. So, Anna had gone to the local chocolate shop, got the most over-the-top box she could find and dropped it off for him that morning at the university, just to teach him a lesson. He walked into the ward where Mike was recovering, feeling horribly self-conscious. Sophie and her parents were sitting next to his bed. He looked subdued and drowsy, and had a large dressing on his right ear.

He smiled weakly when he saw Joseph. "Hey, mate, good to see you. What the hell have you got there?"

"A present from Anna. Well, from all of us, but mainly from Anna. You know." He put the box down on the table at the end of the bed.

Mike grinned. "Thanks. Please tell Anna thanks too."

"How are you feeling now?"

"Not too bad, considering." He motioned Joseph over to where Sophie and her parents were sitting. "You'll need to sit on this side of the bed. Can't hear on the other side too well." Joseph shuffled round to where Sophie, Cliff and Doreen were sitting. "They've still got me lightly sedated so I'm a bit knackered, but otherwise, just feeling very lucky."

Joseph looked at Sophie's parents. The body language said it all. Cliff Sumner was sitting close to Mike, leaning forward and smiling. Doreen Sumner couldn't have looked more different. She sat behind her husband and daughter, making no attempt to talk to Mike and avoiding looking at him. "I'm sorry if I'm interrupting your visit just now. I can come back later."

Doreen stood up. "No, we were just going. Sophie has an ante-natal appointment upstairs in a few minutes. We'll go up with her. Please, do stay and talk to Mike."

Sophie got up and hugged Joseph. "Hey, put him down woman," said Mike. Joseph grinned at him over Sophie's shoulder, playing up the hug with a wink.

As Sophie and her parents left the ward, Joseph sat on one of the chairs at the side of the bed. "I'm glad to see you awake and looking on the mend."

"Yeah, a visit from Sophie's mum is just what I need to cheer me up!"

"A bit difficult, is she?"

"I'm too dark for her taste." Mike smiled. "She's probably disappointed I wasn't killed in the accident."

"Oh, surely not!"

"OK, no, I'm not being fair. But chocolate isn't her favourite treat, that's for sure."

Joseph smiled sympathetically at his friend and moved his chair closer to the bed. He could see bruising beginning to develop around Mike's right eye. "Can you remember what happened?"

"Quite clearly. Gary Mason had brought in this fantastic Winchester and I was shooting it on the range. I shot it a few times, and others had a go too. Then I was shooting a set of repeaters, pulled the trigger one time and blam! I remember the flash and the noise and the pain as the bolt hit me, then nothing until the ambulance crew was getting me onto the stretcher. Bloody guns, eh?"

"Do they know why it exploded?"

"I haven't heard yet, but my guess would be a blockage in the barrel. It might have been a slightly over-sized bullet or something like that. Accidents like this do happen sometimes, particularly with old guns."

"Has he been to see you?" asked Joseph.

"Who, Gary?"

"Yeah."

"No, probably too embarrassed. And there'll be an accident investigation, so he'll be nervous about that, I expect."

Joseph looked behind him to check that no one was in hearing distance, and then leaned a little closer to Mike. "Look, this is going to sound odd, but bear with me. I was chatting with Raman earlier and he mentioned that he's supervising Egraine Mountford now."

Mike nodded.

"He also said that she'd started to come onto him. Did she do anything like that with you? She looked a bit dolled up when she came to see you last week."

Mike looked momentarily shocked, and then put his head in his hands. Joseph waited for him to speak, with a growing sense of dread. "You didn't, did you?" he asked at last.

Mike nodded, still cradling his bandaged head.

"What the hell were you thinking?" Joseph hissed.

"I wasn't. It all happened so quickly. She asked me round to her flat to see the notes and models she'd been working on." He looked up. Joseph gave him an unsympathetic look. "I know, I shouldn't have gone, but she was so persistent. I tell you man, at the time I wanted her so bad. Now I feel sick when I think about her. I emailed her the next morning and told her I couldn't supervise her. I've got no intention of doing anything like that again. I'll see her as little as possible while we finish the work on Nimue." Then realisation dawned. "Oh God, I've lost that chance, haven't I?"

Joseph put his hand on Mike's shoulder. "One step at a time, mate. One step at a time. Just concentrate on getting well for now. Opportunities have a habit of coming round again to those that deserve them."

They sat in silence for a moment, then Mike said, "Did you say she's been coming on to Raman?"

"Yeah. And he made another point too. He said he hoped it was third time lucky for him, as she seems to be jinxed. First Alec, now you. He made out he was joking, but something about what he said has left me wondering."

"But Egraine had nothing to do with my accident, and she's not in the frame for Alec's death." Mike lay back on his pillows, suddenly looking tired. "I think the sedative's beginning to kick in again. I can't take all this in."

"Look, I'm sorry to ask you about it. It's none of my business, but it just seems ... I don't know ... fishy somehow."

Mike started to drift. "It was a stupid mistake. Don't tell Sophie."

"Of course not! Hey, you look shattered. I'll let you get some rest and see you again soon. " He patted Mike on the arm, got up and turned to go, knowing that he would have to tell Kelly about Mike and Egraine. That might be as bad as telling Sophie in the long run. The police would have to investigate it, and then it would all come out. And what if he were wrong? Then Mike and Sophie would suffer all that pain for nothing.

"Joe."

He turned back and leaned over Mike's bed.

"What mate?"

Mike could hardly keep his eyes open. "Gary and Egraine."

"Gary?"

"Something he said. What I think ..." His eyes fluttered as he slid into a sedated sleep.

Joseph walked out of the hospital quickly and almost ran over to his car. He took out his mobile phone and called the lab. Lily answered. "Hi Lily, it's Joseph Connor here. I've just been to see Mike and I wondered if you and Ben would be free for a coffee at, say, three o'clock? Great. I'll see you in the Java Man."

If he was going to get the police to take his next suspicion seriously, he'd need to do some background work first, and Lily and Ben would be a good place to start.

27

A light rain pattered against the window as they sat on uncomfortable 'comfy chairs' at a low table.

"Thanks for coming," said Joseph. "I just wanted to catch up with progress on Nimue. Alec had been so excited by her and I wondered if you'd got any further in the past few weeks? I know Egraine is getting on with sorting out another supervisor. She's asked Raman Sharples, so I know she'll be well looked after. I didn't want you two to feel unsupported, with Mike now being out of circulation."

Ben slurped his coffee and looked over the top of the foam with his eyebrows raised.

"What?" asked Joseph.

"Knowing Egraine I think she'll work her way through the male members of staff here one by one. You'd better watch out Doctor Connor."

"Ben!" Lily gave him a dirty look.

"It's true. I know you don't want to hear it about your friend, but take it from a man. I know a prick teaser when I see one."

"I'm sorry Doctor Connor, you'll have to excuse Ben. He can't help it, he's a twat." She sipped her coffee. "Egraine does like older men, it's true, but she's not as bad as Ben makes out."

Joseph laughed. "OK, I didn't mean to set you both off on one. I just wanted to make sure you were OK, I guess. This is the first research post for both of you after getting your PhDs. It must have been a terrible shock to lose Alec, and now Mike's out of commission. I don't suppose this is what you expected."

"No," agreed Ben. "Alec was a bit of a cold fish, but I actually liked the guy. I know some people didn't, but he was always pretty straight with me. Mike seems like a good guy too."

"I liked Alec too, once I got used to him," agreed Lily. "We didn't know Mike very well, but he seems to be a decent guy and a gifted palaeontologist. Did you know his mother worked for the National Museums of Kenya with the Leakeys! I was so impressed when I found that out."

Joseph was wondering how he could get the subject of Egraine back into the conversation. "It's a run of really bad luck to lose both your project directors to violent acts so close together. You must be feeling pretty unsettled about it all."

"To tell you the truth, I'm beginning to get a weird feeling when I look at Nimue now," said Lily, pulling her fleece around herself tightly.

"What, you think it's cursed or something?" asked Ben sarcastically.

"She, not it." Lily shot him another dirty look, but didn't deny it.

Joseph smiled at them. "Well, I'm sure Alec didn't think she's cursed. He had no time for anything psychic or spiritual."

"No, for all his faults you did get a stable feeling working with Alec. I liked him for that," agreed Lily.

Now was Joseph's chance. "What about Egraine. Do you think she liked him?"

She nodded. "Yes, she did. Actually, I think she had a little crush on him. She's coped with his death very well, considering."

"And what about Alec. Do you think he reciprocated?" asked Joseph.

"I think they were working on something together," said Ben. "I got a bit pissed off 'cos I'm sure we, Lily and me, were being cut out. I don't know what it was, but they kept going off together when we were in Africa and having long and intense conversations. I thought they were shagging, but Lily reckoned not." He turned and looked at her. "Didn't you?"

"Nicely put, as ever. No, actually, I don't think they were 'shagging'. It was something about Alec's behaviour. It didn't seem like he was in that kind of relationship with Egraine. And anyway, he was her supervisor, so I didn't see anything unusual in them having private meetings. I think 'going off together' is making too much of it."

Ben took a last large gulp of his remaining coffee and picked up his rucksack. "Sorry Doctor Connor, but I have to go. I'm teaching a research student tutor group in about twenty minutes, and it's conveniently in a room about as far away from this end of the campus as you can get. Thanks for thinking about us. And for the coffee."

"No problem Ben. I need to be getting on with things too. If either of you need any help, well, you know where I am."

Lily looked for a moment as if she wanted to say something, but then changed her mind.

"Anything bothering you Lily?" asked Joseph.

She hesitated again, just for a microsecond, then said "No, no. Everything's fine." She stood up. "Thanks Doctor Connor. I feel I could talk to you if I ever needed to." She followed Ben out of the Java Man, her fleece still pulled tightly around her.

28

It was late Monday afternoon as Kelly and Robson drove to Juliet's house. They had both had time to think about the Panolbion revelations over the weekend, and to try to make some sense out of what might be going on. Kelly in particular had wanted a couple of days to think. She had no intention of repeating the embarrassing mistake she had made with Thackray. No rushing in this time. If any of the Thackray family were involved in Whickham's death she would have to be careful. And clever. They all seemed to have inherited fierce intellects, whatever their mental states.

Juliet opened the front door and smiled at them weakly. "Please, come in." Kelly felt sympathy for Juliet, but she wasn't sure why. Thackray irritated her enormously, and although she still felt sure that he was implicated in Alec Whickham's death, she couldn't help feeling more positively inclined towards Juliet. "Would you like some tea? Or coffee?" They both shook their heads. Juliet motioned them to sit.

Kelly started in a measured voice. "There are some things we'd like to talk to you about regarding your uncle, Luke Thackray." She watched closely for the reaction, but Juliet was hard to read.

"Uncle Luke? Why?"

"Have you spoken to your uncle since Alec Whickham's death?"

"No. I haven't had any contact with him for over a year. We occasionally meet at family gatherings, but that's all."

"Well, some creationist comments appeared on Doctor. Whickham's blog a couple of weeks before he died. They've been traced back to a computer that appears to have been used by your uncle at the times all four of those comments were made. The last comment has, well, I guess you could call it a bit threatening. And now we've discovered that some of the comments are quotes from a pamphlet call Panolbion. The same name as your uncle's house."

"Quotations. Quote is more correctly used as a verb. The terms are somewhat interchangeable, but it is generally better to use the correct noun to avoid ambiguity." Juliet seemed to be in a sort of trance.

"What?" Kelly looked baffled for a moment. Of all the reactions she expected, correcting her grammar wasn't one of them.

Juliet seemed slightly startled by Kelly's voice. "Oh, I'm sorry. Just a reflex." She smiled weakly again. "I've been doing some thesis marking and I seem to have got into grammar correction mode." She leaned back in her chair wearily. "You'll have to excuse me. I'm not sleeping well, despite some quite powerful sleeping tablets from my doctor. I seem to find concentration difficult." She rubbed her face with the palms of her hands, dislodging her glasses.

Kelly couldn't shake the sense of sympathy she felt for Juliet, but she had a job to do and she was going to do it. "Do you know anything about the blog comments, Professor Bailey?"

"No, nothing." Juliet was still rubbing her eyes.

Kelly decided to try a different tack. "He's an interesting person, your uncle. He was very keen to show us his family tree last time we saw him."

Juliet seemed to relax a little more, and even managed a chuckle as she replaced her glasses. "Ah, yes. The seventh son of a seventh son. He's very excited about all that. Even though one of his uncles died when just a few days old, he still feels it's legitimate to consider himself as a seventh son squared!" Juliet gazed out of the window at the tree blossom. "He wasn't so pleased when he found out the whole story though. I bet he didn't tell you about that."

Kelly took her copy of the Thackray family tree from the back of her notebook and unfolded it onto the coffee table in front of them. "Is this not the whole story then?"

Juliet leaned forward and pointed to the top of the diagram. "May Ellison. The illegitimate daughter of an African slave mother and a plantation owner, William Ellison, who was a freed slave himself. Surprisingly he wasn't the most enlightened plantation owner, but it seems he felt a special empathy with May so it is generally presumed that he was her father. And she took his last name, although that wasn't too uncommon so it doesn't prove anything conclusively. Anyhow, I came across May some years ago, when I was still called Thackray. Someone in the U.S. with the same surname saw a paper I had written and contacted me. She'd been doing some genealogy and had come across the May Ellison story. She sent me a copy of a letter written in 1838 which referred to the daughter of an African female slave and a freed slave plantation owner. It turned out that this was May." Juliet sat back again, looking exhausted by the exertion of talking.

"So you have African ancestry," said Robson.

Juliet smiled. "Every human does, Sergeant. It's where we all came from. That's the real irony of Uncle Luke's bigotry. The ancestors of everyone with a white ethnic heritage walked out of Africa about seventy thousand years ago, give or take. But Africa is where we all started. It's where we learned to walk on two legs, speak, laugh. Do all the things that humans do. It's a story written in our DNA."

"So your uncle took the news of his African ancestor badly?" asked Kelly.

"Oh very!" Juliet's smile broadened. "On several counts. He hates the notion that there's illegitimacy in the family. And, as you say, he really hates the idea of African ancestors. He's a bigoted man, which I think partly accounts for his delusions of grandeur. He's trying to compensate for a flawed family tree! He likes order, purity, that kind of thing." Juliet's distaste for her uncle was clear from the look on her face.

Kelly was beginning to see through the fog. "So that's why he doesn't like the 'out of Africa' theory of human evolution?"

"Yes indeed. Creationism works for him more on personal grounds than from a religious point of view. Deep down he isn't a very religious man. He has a thing about venerating William of Ockham, but that's really more philosophical than religious."

Kelly looked Juliet directly in the eyes. "Would he kill Alec Whickham?"

Juliet looked straight back. "I can see that the coincidence of my ID card being used to open G0 twelve and Uncle Luke sending sinister messages to Alec quoting religious texts might look overly coincidental, but..." She closed her eyes. "Oh God, this is a nightmare." She opened them and looked at Kelly and Robson in despair. "What is going on? Did Uncle Luke really write those blog comments?"

"We'll find out," said Kelly, standing up. "You look very tired so we'll leave you to rest. Just one last question before we go. Did Doctor Whickham tell you anything about his findings as he was reconstructing Nimue's skull?"

Juliet snorted. "No. I'd be the last person Alec would have discussed his work with, particularly in the last few weeks of his life. Communicating with him had become even more difficult for me than usual. Why? What did he find?"

"Nothing of any importance just now," replied Kelly, watching for clues in Juliet's response again. But shet was so groggy with the sleeping tablets her reactions were cloaked. Kelly opened the lounge door. "Please don't get up, we'll let ourselves out."

Juliet nodded, her eyes half shut, as they closed the front door behind them.

"You've got to feel sorry for the poor woman," said Kelly, as they got into the car. "I mean, I've seen plenty of play acting in my time, but she looks like someone on the edge to me. We need to get to the bottom of this case before we have another death on our hands."

"You think she'd top herself?" asked Robson.

"I don't know. I do know that the closer we seem to move towards a solution to this case, the faster it seems to run away from us. We need divine intervention."

Just then her mobile rang. She looked at the screen. *Ah, the divine Doctor Connor. He'll do.*

"Doctor Connor. How are you?"

"I'm fine. You?"

"Not so bad. What's up?"

"Did you hear about Mike Osewe? He's been injured in a shooting accident at the university rifle range."

Kelly was shocked. "Oh dear. I'm very sorry to hear that. How is he?"

"I've just been to see him in hospital and he's dazed, but at least he's alive and likely to make a good recovery. Minus an ear, though."

Kelly grimaced. "Oh no."

"Look, there's something I'm really concerned about. I think Mike's injury might be connected to Alec's death in some way. Can I come and talk to you now?"

"We could meet in the coffee shop. Same one as last time. I could be there in about…" She looked at Robson and he mouthed 'ten'. "… ten minutes."

"OK, see you there." The divine Doctor Connor rang off.

29

Kelly was waiting at a corner table when Joseph walked in.

"My round, I think," she said, standing up and gesturing for him to sit down. "What would you like?"

"Oh, actually, I've not long had one. Just a tea thanks."

"My pleasure."

She walked over to the counter and ordered Joseph his tea and herself a double chocolate macchiato with whipped cream. For some reason she was feeling girlish today.

Joseph leaned over when she sat back down at the table. "I wanted to talk about Mike. About his injury."

"Not our province I don't think. You said it was an accident."

"Yes, it looks that way but, well, I think it may be connected to Alec's death."

"What makes you think that?" asked Kelly.

"Egraine Mountford, Alec's research student. I guess you interviewed her?"

"Yes, we interviewed her, Ben whassisname and the other researcher, Lily White. Great name. Anyway, they all had alibis. OK, so White and Mountford gave each other alibis, it's true, but we did get corroboration from the people in the neighbouring flat who said they heard them all evening. The walls are paper thin, apparently. Anyway, they didn't have any obvious motive, or the means to do it."

"At Alec's funeral Egraine asked Mike to be her PhD supervisor. When they met the next day to talk it through she invited him back to her flat and, well, not to put too fine a point on it, she seduced him."

Kelly grinned. "No law against that. He's an attractive man."

"Yes, and in a stable relationship with a pregnant partner."

Kelly shrugged. "Still not illegal." They got the call for their drinks at that moment, and went to pick them up. Kelly's came in a tall glass and looked more like an ice cream sundae than a drink. Joseph looked at her quizzically. "In a playful mood today?"

"Mmm, even police officers can have a bit of fun you know." They went back to the table.

"OK, listen," said Joseph. "Firstly, according to Lily and Ben, Egraine had a bit of a thing about Alec but he wasn't interested in her romantically. He dies. Then she has a bit of a thing about Mike. They have one brief fling and then he tells her he doesn't want to see her again. He nearly gets his head blown off. She then asks another good looking man in his late thirties, Raman Sharples, to supervise her. Now Raman tells me that she's been flirting with him, pretty seriously."

Kelly put on a creditable Miss Piggy impersonation. "I'm beginning to see a pattern in the men I date." She giggled. "Muppet Treasure Island. Great film."

Joseph didn't laugh. "I'm deadly serious. And I think Egraine might be too."

It was clear that he wasn't going to play with her so she gave up and looked at her coffee with regret. "But we can't tie her to either Doctor

Whickham's death or Doctor Osewe's injury. She wasn't there either time."

"No, but a student named Gary Mason may have been. He was certainly there when Mike was injured, and something Mike said today when I saw him at the hospital made me wonder."

"What did he say?"

"Well, just 'Gary and Egraine'. He was woozy with the sedatives and on the edge of passing out so he didn't elaborate. But why would he associate the two of them? Maybe it's worth checking them out, just to see if there is any link between them," said Joseph, although now he had told Kelly, it didn't sound anything like as convincing as when it had just been in his head.

"OK, I'll get checks run on them, but I do think it's all a bit thin. There's no evidence that Mountford had any involvement in Alec Whickham's death. And, your record on hunches isn't too reliable, is it? Your last one about the blog postings still hasn't come to anything. Despite my best efforts," she added, somewhat ruefully.

"I know, but this time I've got a much more distinct feeling."

"As I've said before, Doctor Connor, I can't go on feelings."

"But it would be odd if there were an association, don't you think?"

"It all sounds coincidental to me. The activities of one randy student don't amount to motives for murder and attempted murder. But I'll get the two of them checked out, if you promise to stop playing detective. I have asked you that once before."

"Yes, I know. Of course, sure, I won't do anything."

"Good. Right, I've got to go." She got up and turned towards the door.

"You haven't touched your coffee," said Joseph.

She turned back. "No, somehow I've lost the mood. Promise me, no investigating. Whoever is responsible for Alec Whickham's death is not someone you want to tangle with. And if they're also involved in Mike's injury, they could be very dangerous indeed."

Joseph nodded. "Don't worry, I'll behave."

Fat chance, she thought, as she walked out of the cafe and into the fresh spring rain.

30

Joseph picked up his jacket from the stand in the hall. "See you later," he shouted.

"'Bye love," came Anna's response from upstairs.

He got into the car, wondering why the hell he was doing this. But he was sure about one thing. Egraine had something to do with Alec's death and Mike's accident. He didn't think that Kelly was going to take him seriously this time though, particularly as his suspicions about the postings on Alec's blog had come to nothing. He had promised Kelly yesterday that he wouldn't get involved, but if he could just get Egraine to spill something about her relationships with Alec and Mike, perhaps he would get Kelly's full attention next time. And, maybe Egraine would try something on with him if he made out he was interested in her work, which might flush her out. So, he had arranged to see Egraine at her flat this evening. He knew he might be playing a dangerous game, in more ways than one, but Alec and Mike were his friends and he owed it to them. Not to mention Juliet, still locked away in her house going slowly mad.

He parked in the local centre car park near the flats in Rufus Court. This was where he usually parked on his visits to Juliet, who lived just round the corner. He crossed the road and walked the two hundred yards or so to Egraine's flat. He knocked on the door and she opened it, wearing baggy jeans, a loose top and a pair of large, bunny-rabbit slippers. She had her hair pulled back into a pony tail, reading glasses perched on the top of her head and her face looked scrubbed and shiny. *Oh well, at least I don't appear to be a seduction target.*

"Hi, Doctor Connor. Come in." She led Joseph down the hall and into the lounge. Papers, artefacts and balsa models were strewn all over the lounge table and a half-drunk bottle of white wine, cork out, was balanced on top of a pile of papers on the floor. "Sorry, you'll have to excuse the mess, I'm working on my thesis."

"This looks like really interesting stuff. The models are particularly good."

"Thanks. Well, they're not completely accurate anatomically – they're more like vehicles for me to try out some ideas." She motioned for him to sit down.

"I wanted to see how you are," Joseph said. "We haven't had chance to talk much since that terrible day in the lab, and now you've lost Mike as the project leader too. As Raman says, this whole project is beginning to look jinxed! I met with Lily and Ben yesterday and they seem to be coping well. How are you doing?"

She looked concerned. "It's all been very stressful and worrying, to be honest. I'm really concerned that the Kenyan authorities will want Nimue back right now, and I couldn't blame them. We'll lose the chance to work on her and that would make my research contract with the university look precarious. And Lily and Ben too. At least they've got their doctorates. Have you any idea how difficult it is to get paid studentships? Oh, yes, sorry, of course you do." She put her head in her hands. "I liked Alec and Mike personally too, so it's been really upsetting." She pulled herself up. "But, Raman is being very helpful and supportive. Everyone is, actually." She looked at him and smiled.

If this is an act, it's a very good one, thought Joseph. He began to think that this visit was a wild goose chase. Maybe if he tried to make the situation look bleak she would rise to it a bit more. "I know that the university will be trying to negotiate with the Kenyan authorities, but we're running out of people to lead this project. With Juliet looking likely to be found guilty, Alec gone and Mike likely to be out of commission for some time, it's hard to see who's left to pick it up."

"Raman could, couldn't he?" she asked, hopefully.

"Well, it's not really his field, and he may not have the experience that the Kenyans are looking for." She began to look more agitated. "This was Alec's project." He continued to press the point home. "Anyone else is just a stand-in. Mike's my friend, but he wasn't really up to this, if I'm honest. And Raman certainly isn't. Alec had that touch of genius that only comes along rarely. Whoever killed him did a terrible thing, not just to him and his family, but to this project and the furtherance of our understanding of ourselves." He looked hard into her eyes and saw only sadness there.

"That's so true," she replied, and sniffed. She pulled a scrunched-up tissue from her sleeve and blew her nose. "But I'm forgetting my manners. Would you like a drink?" The sudden change of subject took Joseph by surprise, but he recovered quickly. "A coffee would be good, thanks."

She got up and went into the kitchen. He heard the sound of water running. Music suddenly started playing from somewhere in the room, and it took him a moment or two to realise that it was her mobile phone on the coffee table in front of him. She came back into the room and picked it up.

"Hi. Not right now but we could do later. I'll call you. Bye." She smiled at Joseph and went back into the kitchen.

He didn't know why, but he picked up her phone and pressed last call. The name stared out at him from the screen.

Gary.

Joseph was sweating. *Oh God, what have I got myself into?* He knew he was out of his depth and needed to get out of Egraine's flat as soon as he could. He took his own mobile out of his pocket and switched it on, hardly noticing the missed call from Kelly.

"Oh, sorry Egraine," he said, standing up as she came back into the room with the coffee. "I've just had a call from my wife. I need to get back right now. A bit of a domestic crisis. Don't worry, I'll let myself out." He almost ran down the hall and out of the door. Egraine put the coffee down on the table and saw that her mobile was showing 'last caller'. She picked it up and pressed call.

31

It was seven o'clock and Kelly was packing up for the evening when Robson came back to his desk. "Those checks on Mountford and Mason have come back."

"What have we got then? Anything interesting?"

"Not really. No known association between them." He skimmed the paperwork. "Egraine Mountford, twenty three years old, daughter of William and Helena Mountford. He's a civil servant. The family travelled all over the place from the look of it. He's currently working in Egypt. Helena Mountford died eight years ago. Gary Mason, nineteen, son of Hilary Mason. Father not known. Born and brought up in Falkirk. I can't see any family connection between them, but I suppose they may be in a relationship. Although we checked both their Facebook sites and neither of them lists the other as a friend as far as I can see. We got Mountford's mobile phone details when we interviewed her at first, so I've got call records being checked too, for completeness. Should get those back shortly, but it doesn't look like there's any connection between them so far."

"OK, so, looks like another of Doctor Connor's hunches isn't going play out." She leaned back in her chair. "That just leaves us with Juliet Bailey. There's really no one else in the frame. Thackray doesn't have an alibi, but neither does he have any real motive, nor a clear opportunity to kill Whickham. There's no real case against him, unfortunately." She paused, then asked, "Gary Mason didn't have any connection with Alec Whickham, did he?"

Robson shook his head. "Nope, he's a second year student in computing. He's not even on the same part of the campus."

Kelly looked thoughtful. "He's a computing student?"

"Yes, so what?"

"Go and see him tomorrow. Find out if he has an alibi for the night Alec Whickham was killed."

"What are you driving at?" asked Robson.

At that moment a young constable came to their desks. "Excuse me ma'am, but I've just got the mobile phone records for Egraine Mountford. She's made four calls to a mobile number registered to a Gary Mason in the past three months. The last one was at nine twenty-four pm on the tenth of April."

Kelly stood up quickly. "Come on Jack, we have to find Mason and Mountford and get them in here as fast as we can." She pulled out her mobile phone and scanned through the recent calls directory until she found Joseph. She made the call. "Come on Joseph. Answer it."

"This is Joseph Connor. Leave me a message and I'll get back to you."

"Doctor Connor, could you call me as soon as you get this message please? It's urgent. Thanks." She rang off. "Emma, would you get me Joseph Connor's home phone number, please?"

"Why are you calling Connor?" asked Robson.

"Because I think he may be daft enough to get himself killed."

They walked across the office to where DC Emma Waters was looking at her computer screen. "Got it ma'am."

Kelly tapped the number into her mobile and Anna's voice answered. Kelly hesitated. "Oh, hello Mrs Connor. Is Doctor Connor there please? It's DI Kelly."

"No, I'm sorry. He's gone over to see one of Alec's research students. He'll be back later. Can I get him to call you?"

Kelly went cold, but battled to sound matter-of-fact. "Er, yes please. Did he happen to mention the name of the student he was going to see?"

"Yes, Egraine, I think he said."

"Ah, OK, I see. No problem. If you could ask him to call me on my mobile if .." she corrected herself quickly, "…I mean when he gets back. Thanks very much." Kelly rang off. "Shit. We need to get round to Mountford's flat right now. Have you got the address?"

"Yep." Robson picked up his jacket from the back of his chair.

"I'll try his mobile again on the way. Come on, step on it then!"

Joseph ran out of Egraine's flat and along the road, heading back towards the car park. A car on the opposite side of the road started its engine and revved up loudly. Joseph saw the headlights reflecting in the shop windows as it did a U-turn and headed straight for him. He could feel his heart racing as he sped down the road towards the corner.

His mobile rang. *Sod it, not now!* He ignored it and carried on running as he heard the car screaming towards him. Then another one came around the corner in front of him. He just had time to recognise it as Robson's as the car behind hit him and sent him flying over the bonnet.

Robson braked hard and Kelly jumped out. "Follow him!" she shouted, as she ran over to where Joseph lay. He wasn't moving. "Oh you silly sod, why couldn't you do as you were told!" She pulled her mobile out of her bag and called for an ambulance. "There's been a serious road accident. It's DI Kelly. Corner of Wellington Road and Rufus Drive. Get them here quick." She kneeled down and stroked his forehead, feeling the sticky sensation of blood. "Come on Joseph, stay with me. Please."

The car in front was an old, clapped out Ford Escort that was pouring out grey smoke from the exhaust. Robson put his foot flat to the floor and shot the red light at the junction with Redfern Road. *He can't keep this up for long. His car's going to give out any minute.* The Escort screamed down Rufus Drive in front of him and headed towards the sea. *Oh, shit. Too fast, too fast! He's never going to make the turn onto the Promenade!* The lights changed to amber; the Escort's tyres squealed as the car tried to make a sharp left turn. But Robson's intuition was right. It was going too fast. It flipped over, bouncing bonnet over boot, and careened into the railings at the sea front. There was a high spring tide and the waves were smacking into the sea wall, spraying the road with foam and froth. The railings gave way as the car somersaulted into the sea, its headlights carving a bright white arc across the ominous sky. Robson screeched to a halt, got out of his car and ran over to the sea wall. The car was upside down in more than four feet of water. He couldn't hope to reach the driver. Taking his torch from the glove compartment he shone it on the crashed car, illuminating the driver's smashed window. He could see a body through the churning water, hanging upside down from the seatbelt. A thick liquid line traced a scarlet watermark in the white foam.

32

The scene was fuzzy and indistinct. Gradually the room began to come into focus. Anna; there was Anna. Looking drawn and tear stained, but definitely Anna. And Mark and Jenny. His eyes opened wider and the picture began to resolve, like a squeegee being pulled across a wet window.

"Oh Joseph, can you hear me?!" Anna dissolved into tears as he squeezed her hand and nodded. He didn't feel any pain, just a vague light-headedness. He wished the room would stop rotating though. And that everyone would stop whispering to each other. He closed his eyes again, tuning out the susurration around the bed. After a few minutes he began to feel more stable. When he opened his eyes this time things kept still, by and large. He saw that his left arm and leg were plastered. He turned his head a little further to the left and saw Mike, sitting in a wheelchair next to the bed. He had a drip attached and was still heavily bandaged around his head. They smiled at each other, and then Joseph had the overwhelming urge to laugh; he knew it was totally inappropriate, but it was also completely overwhelming. It was so ridiculous. How could they have got into this situation? Anna looked terrified as he started to chuckle, but then Mike got the joke and joined in too. They laughed as much as their broken bodies would let them and then the wave passed as quickly as it had started. The mood was lifted though, and everyone around the bed visibly relaxed.

"Dad, how do you feel?" It was Jenny.

"Woozy, but not too bad love."

"What do you remember Joseph?" The voice came from his right. He turned to see Kelly sitting at the side of the bed, looking crumpled and bleary-eyed.

"Er, well, I remember being in Egraine's flat. Her mobile rang, and when I looked it said Gary. I thought it might be Gary, er, thingy, what's his name?"

"Mason."

"Yeah, Mason. Sorry, I'm still a bit fuzzy. I remember feeling like I needed to get out of the flat, but that's all. What happened to me?"

"You were hit by a car being driven by Gary Mason." She took her mobile out of her bag and speed dialled Robson. "Jack. Joseph's awake. It looks like Mason phoned Mountford a few minutes before he hit Joseph. We've got enough on her to arrest her and bring her in for questioning. And get round to see her friend, Lily White, about that alibi. I don't buy it. Mountford definitely called Mason the night Alec Whickham was killed. Our Doctor White has got to know more than she's saying. I'm going home to get a few hours sleep, but I'll be back in this afternoon" She rang off.

Anna looked sick. "This was deliberate?"

"I believe so. We haven't put it all together yet, but I think we're finally getting somewhere in this whole case. Alec Whickham, Mike and Joseph. They're all connected, and that connection is Egraine Mountford, I'm sure of it. Now we have to find out how and why." She shot a quick smile of understanding at Mike and then turned to Joseph. "I'm so sorry that I didn't react more quickly when you came to see me about Mountford and Mason."

Joseph shook his head and immediately winced at the pain in his neck. "No, my fault. You warned me and I went ahead and did it anyway." He looked at her more closely. "You look shattered."

Anna squeezed his hand. "Inspector Kelly has been here with us all night. She saw the accident and called the ambulance."

"I needed to ask you what had happened as soon as you woke up." Kelly looked slightly embarrassed as she rose from her chair. "Mission accomplished, so I'll leave you to your family and friends. We'll probably need to talk to you again at some stage, but for now, just get better." She patted him on his good arm, nodded to the rest of the people around the bed and turned to go.

"Have you got Gary?" asked Mike.

"Yes," replied Kelly, turning back. "But he won't help us."

"Why not?"

"Because he's dead."

Lily looked frightened and close to tears. "I can't believe you've arrested Egraine. She wouldn't hurt anyone."

Robson didn't reply. He clicked the record button on the machine and said "Interview with Doctor Lily White at eleven thirty-five on the thirtieth of April. Doctor White has declined legal representation at this time."

Lily blew her nose on a tissue and put it back up her sleeve.

"I'd like you to tell me again about your movements on the evening of April the tenth," said Robson.

"I was at Egraine's flat all evening. We were watching TV."

"Were you both there all evening?"

"Yes."

"Neither of you left at any time?"

She hesitated and bit the end of her right thumb. "No."

"So you heard the phone call Egraine made to Gary Mason, then?"

"What phone call?" Lily looked very frightened now.

"Doctor White, I'll ask you one more time. Did Egraine leave the flat at any time that night?"

Tears began to well at the corners of her eyes. "Yes. She went out to get a bottle of wine from the all night store around the corner. But she was only gone for ten minutes at the most. Honestly, she only had enough time to get to the shop and come back." Robson pursed his lips and looked at Lily's previous statement. "You didn't mention this at your last interview. Why not?"

"I forgot. Honestly. I wasn't trying to hide anything. Truly, she was gone for ten minutes. It was nothing like the time she would have needed to even get to the labs, let alone do anything when she got there. When I remembered later, I didn't know whether to tell anyone. I didn't know if it mattered. She was out for such a short time. "

"It was long enough to make a phone call."

"Sorry?"

"Never mind. What time did she go to the shop?"

"It must have been around twenty past nine."

"And can you remember when she got back?"

"About ten minutes later, just as the film started. Must have been nine thirty." Lily dabbed her eyes with a tissue. "What's Egraine got to do with all this?"

"That's what we're trying to find out."

Kelly arrived at the station at three pm, looking and feeling much better after a shower and three or four hours sleep.

Robson filled her in. "Lily White confirms that Mountford left the flat at around nine twenty and came back ten minutes later. I don't think that she hid that deliberately the first time round. It was just such a short length of time she forgot. When she did remember, she didn't think it was important."

"So Mountford went out to make a call to Mason. We can be pretty sure of that. But why?"

"I don't know. Perhaps we should ask her. She's been stewing in one of the cells for a couple of hours now. I've made sure she doesn't know anything about what happened to Mason."

"Well then, another hour or so won't hurt. We've still got time. I want to walk the route from her flat to the shop before we question her."

They walked out to the car park and Robson took up his customary position behind the wheel. He started the engine and reversed out. "So," he asked, nonchalantly. "How's Doctor Connor looking?"

"Lucky, more than anything. He has some broken bones on his left side, but it could have been much worse."

He shot her a sideways glance.

"You like him, don't you?"

Kelly blushed. "Oh grow up, Jack."

Robson smiled to himself. When they reached Rufus Court he parked in the local centre car park. They crossed the road, past where Joseph had been hit, and walked round to number ten A.

"OK," said Kelly. "The obvious route to the shop is along the edge of these flats and round into Wellington Drive. I have a hunch, so let's see if it holds up." They started timing and walked the route; three minutes later they found themselves outside Juliet Bailey's house. "Aha, so that is it."

"What?" asked Robson.

"She was checking if Bailey was in. If they planned to frame her, Mason needed to kill Alec Whickham at a time when she was in the house alone. "

"Mason killed Alec Whickham?"

"Yes, I believe he did. But he didn't plan it. I think our PhD student was the brains behind this. I'm still not clear on motive, though. Right, come on, let's see how long it takes us to walk round to the shop, buy something and then get back to Mountford's flat." It took them eleven and a half minutes to buy a packet of cigarettes for Robson and get back to Egraine's front door.

"Right, I think she's waited long enough," said Kelly. "Let's get back and start questioning her. This could be another long night."

33

Egraine sat in the interview room with a mug of tea steaming in front of her. Her solicitor sat by her side.

"You have eaten something, have you?" asked Kelly.

She nodded.

"And you're OK with that tea?"

Another nod.

Kelly and Robson sat down opposite her and Kelly pressed the record button on the small black machine at the side of the table. She spoke to the room in general. "This interview will be recorded and conducted under the Police and Criminal Evidence Act 1984. Detective Inspector Kelly and Detective Sergeant Robson interviewing Miss Egraine Mountford, at four thirty pm on the thirtieth of April. Miss Mountford has chosen to be accompanied by her solicitor, Mr Edward Baker." Kelly looked at Egraine. "Egraine Mountford, you do not have to say anything, but it may harm your defence if you do not mention when questioned something which you later rely on in court. Anything you do say may be given in evidence."

Egraine picked up her mug of tea with both hands and sipped it.

"Do you understand your rights?" asked Kelly.

She nodded.

"Could you speak for the recording please?"

"Yes, I understand."

"You're here under suspicion of involvement in the murder of Doctor Alec Whickham and the serious injuries inflicted on Doctor Michael Osewe and Doctor Joseph Connor."

"I don't understand why," she replied.

"We know you and Gary did this. We just don't know how or why," said Robson, leaning over the table.

"Gary who?"

"Gary Mason."

"Gary Mason? That's ridiculous. I barely know him."

"Come on Egraine, we have your mobile phone records. We know the two of you phoned each other quite regularly."

Egraine sighed. "Hardly regularly. And anyway, how does that mean I had anything to do with Alec's murder? And what could I possibly have to do with Mike and Doctor Connor's accidents? I was nowhere near either of them at the time."

"Through your association with Gary."

She put her mug down on the table and hugged herself. Her eyes began to look damp. "Really and truly, I liked Alec and Mike, and Doctor Connor. They're good people. I didn't want to hurt anyone. Why would I?"

"That's what we need you to tell us."

"Well, I didn't." She looked genuinely upset.

"So you didn't conspire with Gary Mason to kill Alec Whickham and to attempt to kill Michael Osewe and Joseph Connor?"

"No! Honestly, I hardly know him. We met at a party and he's been a bit keen on me since. He got my mobile number a while ago. He's been making a bit of a nuisance of himself to be honest. So I called him to ask him to stop following me and stop pestering me a few times. That's all."

"So, it won't upset you to know that Gary Mason died last night in a road accident?"

Whatever reaction Robson had hoped to get from this statement, he didn't expect what happened next. Nothing. No reaction. Not just no reaction, but a space where there should have been one. Not even common human concern. The light had been switched off.

Confused by her response, or rather the complete lack of one, Robson took a flier. "How long have you been in a relationship with him?" he asked.

She looked at him, threw her head back and laughed. "Oh, many years." Her face hardened suddenly. "He was my brother, you fuckwit. Well, half brother, actually. He was a right little bastard!" She laughed again.

Her solicitor leant forward in alarm. "My client would like a little time to ...", but Egraine interrupted him.

"Oh shut up! What's the saying? Oh yes. I would like to make a statement."

"Look, we've checked Gary Mason's personal details and there's no family connection between you," said Robson. "Try again."

"Bet you didn't get the whole sordid story. Gary Mason. Mother, Hilary Mason, secretary to William Mountford 1985 - 1991. Father, surprise surprise, William Mountford. All dealt with very discreetly; not talked about in decent circles, don't ya know. Broke my mother's heart. She started drinking heavily after it all came out and was dead by the time she was forty-five."

Her solicitor tried again. "I really do think my client needs a little time …"

Egraine turned and looked him straight in the eyes. "Will you shut the fuck up!" He gave up and sat back in his chair.

"How old were you when your mother died?" asked Kelly

Egraine turned her piercing stare towards Kelly and grinned. "Sixteen. Scarred me for life," she said sarcastically. "Turned me into the monster you see today. That and all the physical abuse at the hands of an alcoholic mother. Still, at least it was only on school holidays. The rest of the time they packed me off to boarding school while they lived abroad. Got me well out of the way, like Gary. He was banished to Scotland with his mother. All paid for by my father. She told everyone her husband had died and settled down to raise her little secret as Gary Mason."

"Why did you have Gary kill Alec Whickham?" asked Kelly.

Egraine's face darkened. "He had it coming. Autistic freak."

"Why? What did he do to you?"

"I gave him everything. I researched and wrote the paper that would make his name in mainstream science. No more time in the wilderness. I didn't want any attribution. I did it for him. I loved him and he rejected me in favour of some skanky prostitute. No one does that to me. Gary tried to warn off his tart, but she took no notice."

"And Mike Osewe? What did he do to you?"

"He screwed me and dumped me. No one does that to me either."

"Does everyone have to love you, Egraine?" asked Kelly.

She thought for a few seconds, then shrugged. "Would make a nice change."

"So, how long have you known Gary?"

"About six years. My mother told me all the dirty little secrets a week before she died. I think she wanted to get it all off her chest. Anyhow, I found him a year or so later. Once I knew they were called Mason and lived in Falkirk, it wasn't difficult to find him. We got on very well together. He was so chuffed to find that he had a sister. I didn't tell my father that we knew each other though, and Hilary kept it to herself too. Dad had always stayed in touch with Gary and his mum, but she didn't want her cover blown. By then she was a councillor and getting into local politics. So Gary and I stayed in touch by phone and letters. We didn't do anything online, on Facebook or anything, so no one knew we were related."

"Gary was a student at UNWE too?" asked Robson

"Yes, in computing. He turned out to be quite a whiz with technology. The brains seem to come from my father's side. I was looking for somewhere to do my PhD and Gary wanted to do something with computing technology, so we decided we'd both apply to UNWE so we could see each other more."

"Tell us what happened on the tenth of April, the night Alec Whickham was killed."

She grinned at the memory. "Ah, yes. It all went like clockwork. A very well worked-out plan if I say so myself. I'd got Bailey's ID card a few weeks before and given it to Gary. He copied it and I put it back in her office the following day. Then it was easy. We just waited until an evening when Alec was going to work very late. On that night he wanted to get everything ready for Joseph Connor to see the next day. Pathetic really. He was like a little kid showing his daddy. As soon as I left the lab that particular night I phoned Gary and told him that we'd be going for it tonight. I'd asked Lily over so that I had an alibi. Gary didn't need one as no one would link him to the murder. I did a last minute check that Bailey was at home and phoned Gary. Then he just went into the lab, killed Alec with a stone axe I'd brought back from Africa and then decorated him." She began to giggle. "We couldn't resist it. I'd spent so many days in the lab cleaning those fucking fossilised shellfish. We thought he should wear a crown of them!" She started to laugh loudly.

"Where's the hand axe Egraine?" asked Kelly softly.

"I've still got it." She couldn't stop laughing now. "It was on the table when Mike and Joseph both came over! Right in front of them!"

They waited while she calmed down. "There was blood-stained paper in Professor Bailey's dustbin," said Kelly. "It was Alec Whickham's blood."

"Yep, Gary sneaked into her back garden and put it in her bin." Egraine's eyes were sparkling.

"And why did he kill him with a hand axe?"

Egraine shrugged. "Seemed somehow appropriate."

"Did you know about the wound to the back of Nimue's skull?" asked Kelly.

Egraine looked blank. "What wound?"

"Nothing. Never mind. OK, let's move on to Mike Osewe. What did you and Gary do to him?"

"Ah yes. Mister fuck and run. Another pathetic character. He was easy, too. Gary had met him a few times at the gun club and when he saw what Mike did to me he was only too happy to sacrifice the Winchester rifle our father had given to him secretly the previous year. Dad has a few rifles that he's collected on his travels. He's quite a keen big game hunter." She wrinkled her nose. "Bastard. Anyway, he wanted to give Gary something for his eighteenth birthday and so sent him over an original Winchester. Gary used to load his own ammunition, so it was pretty easy to load an oversize round and give it to Mike."

"Gary actually saw you and Doctor Osewe, did he?" asked Robson, with a bit more interest than was probably appropriate.

Elaine smiled. "Yeah. Well, heard rather than saw. We shared lots of things."

Kelly cut in. "OK, moving on. What about Joseph Connor?"

"That was messy, running Connor over, but, hey, we were improvising by then. You can give us some credit for that. I saw that Connor had checked my phone so he knew that Gary had called me. He was waiting in the car outside. So I just phoned him to tell him Connor was onto us. The rest came naturally to him." She giggled again.

Kelly could sense that she would never get through to Egraine now. Something had changed in her when she found out that Gary had died. But it still rankled with her. "Just because you didn't actually do the deeds, it doesn't mean you aren't guilty, you know. You'll be going to jail for a very long time for your involvement in all this."

"Yeah, whatever. It doesn't really matter now. Any of it. We had a good run. We'd both had enough of being shat on from a great height by people who were supposed to love us. They all had it coming. Gary was the only person I've ever been able to rely on. The only person that ever really loved me. Now he's gone. So nothing matters."

It was dark. Three o'clock in the morning. The duty officer checked her and saw her curled up and still; just a bump under the sheets. He closed the metal shutter on his side of the cell door and his footsteps faded down the corridor. She got up and pulled the bed round slowly and quietly until the metal bed head was under the light fitting. She took off her leggings and tied one leg in a loop and slip knot, taking care to make sure that the loop could pull tight. Balancing on the bed head, she reached up and tied the other leg around the light fitting and checked that it would hold her weight. It was quite tricky to get it through the gap between the fitting and the ceiling, but she had small and dexterous hands. And as much time as she needed. He wouldn't be back for another hour. She pulled the leg through the gap so that the loop was just next to her head, and then tied it off tightly. "Love you, bro," she whispered, as she put her head through the loop and stepped off the bed head.

34

Kelly's phone rang. She woke up blearily and squinted at the red digits on the clock, willing them to come into focus. Quarter to five. *Oh, for God's sake. Who's died?* The thought turned her cold. She rolled over and picked up the phone, suddenly wide awake.

"Yes. What's happened?"

There was a slight hesitation and then she heard the voice of George Edwards, the night duty sergeant.

"Sorry to wake you ma'am, but there's been a serious incident at the station," he said. Another hesitation. "Egraine Mountford has hanged herself. She's been found dead in her cell. I thought we should let you know as soon as possible."

"Oh, thank God," she said. *It wasn't Joseph.*

"Ma'am?"

"I mean oh God, and, er, thank you for calling me so promptly. I'll be there asap." She put the phone down and lay back.

Her immediate relief at the call not being about Joseph evaporated quickly as the reality hit her. A suicide in police custody. She'd thought that her work would be in mounting the case against Egraine, but now it would be dealing with investigations by the Prisons and Probation Ombudsman.

"Shit, shit, shit." She swung her legs over the side of the bed, stood up and stretched. "SHIT!"

The swearing released a bit of the tension, but not very much. She got dressed quickly, pulled her hair back into a pony tail and slapped on a bit of foundation powder and mascara, then picked up her mobile and called Robson's home number. After a few rings a sleepy female voice answered.

"Hello?"

"Oh, hi Paula. It's Elaine. Really sorry to wake you at this hour, but I need to talk to Jack."

"OK. Hang on."

He came on, sounding as dozy as his wife. "What's up?"

Kelly took a deep breath. "Bad news I'm afraid. Egraine Mountford has hanged herself. Found dead in the cells. I'm just on my way in. I think you'd better get over there quick too."

"How the hell did that happen?"

"I haven't got any detail yet, but we need to get over to the station pronto. I'll see you there."

"OK." He rang off.

Kelly got into her car and drove to the station as the sun began to rise over the roofs of the town.

35

It had been a long day, and it wasn't over yet. The PPO's office had been informed of Egraine's death and had already sent a preliminary investigator. Her body had been removed for autopsy, which was due to take place first thing tomorrow morning. Under the circumstances all police actions involving Juliet had been dropped, and Kelly was keen to tell her in person. She took the opportunity to drive over to Juliet's house in the afternoon. It was a good excuse to get out of the station too; Egraine's death had affected her more than she would have thought. *An intelligent person, but so deeply damaged.*

As she drove along the promenade she thought about all the people in this case and how much they had distracted her emotionally. Even Nimue. *Such a familiar crime, but such a vast span of time.* The picture of Nimue and Alec Whickham, side by side, had haunted her since that first day in the lab. And once she knew that they had both been killed in the same way, the sense of futility in her job had become almost overwhelming. *If this is so deeply embedded in human nature, what's the bloody point?* Usually she could stay reasonably objective about her work and the people affected, but not this time. This time everyone had got under her skin. Even someone who had died more than a million years ago. And it had affected her judgement, too; her reaction to Luke Thackray, her feelings for Joseph Connor. *Christ, I've made a real mess of this one. Well at least I've got some good news for Juliet Bailey,* she thought as she drew up in front of Juliet's house. She felt almost elated that she could help Juliet to heal the wounds that the past couple of months had inflicted on her.

She walked to the front door of the house and rang the bell. No answer. She waited for a couple of minutes and then rang it again. Still no reply. With a growing sense of disquiet she tried the handle and found that it moved. She pushed the door open and called down the hall.

"Professor Bailey? It's DI Kelly. Are you there?" No reply. With mounting anxiety she stepped in. "Professor Bailey. Are you OK?"

She heard a small sound, like a sob or gasp, come from the lounge. She ran down the hall and through the open doorway. There was a tray of tea and a large cake on the low table. Juliet was standing by the side of the sofa, looking down at the floor behind it. She turned when she heard Kelly come into the room. The blood was beginning to coagulate on the long knife she was holding, but a small drop fell as she moved. It hit the carpet. Kelly tried to stay calm and matter of fact, despite the sinking sense in her stomach.

"Professor Bailey, what's happened?" she asked in a quiet voice.

Juliet turned back and pointed behind the sofa with the knife. Kelly walked over slowly. Luke Thackray was lying face up on the floor, a deep stab wound gaping from his chest. His eyes were wide open. Kelly bent down and felt for a pulse. Nothing. She stood up slowly.

"Tell me what happened," she asked again.

"It was him," Juliet replied, with absolute conviction. "He killed Alec. He denied it when I asked him, but I know it was him. He did write those blog postings. He finally admitted that." She looked at Kelly with wild hope in her eyes. "You knew it was him, didn't you? You'd never have got him, you know. He's far too slippery. This is the only way. Real justice."

Kelly slipped her hand into her pocket and slowly brought out her mobile phone. "I'll just get someone to come and help you." She walked back down the hall and speed-dialled Robson.

"Jack," she said in a low voice. "Get to Juliet Bailey's house quick. Bring back-up and SOCO. Bailey's killed her uncle. Luke Thackray's dead."

She walked back into the lounge and gently took the cake knife from Juliet, who put up no resistance. Kelly walked her over to the large armchair, sat her down and put the knife on the table, well out of her reach. She tried for the third time. "Juliet, I need you to tell me what happened."

"I knew you'd never get the odious man. So I invited him round for afternoon tea to get him to own up, and we talked for a little. He did own up to posting those comments on Alec's blog, and seemed so very pleased with himself. My life has been turned upside down and he just sat there smiling like a lunatic. The knife was in front of me and I picked it up." She paused and looked confused. "Then you came in just now." Then her eyes brightened. "You know it was him, don't you?"

Kelly felt sick. *How am I going to tell her about Egraine now?* She decided it wasn't the right time and fudged the answer. "We'll sort all that out when we get you to the station. You know you'll have to stand trial for this, don't you?"

Juliet nodded, but said nothing. Strangely, she was smiling.

Kelly stared at the wall. *This is my fault. My bloody conviction about Thackray led to this.*

They sat in mutual silence until Kelly heard Robson's voice in the hall. "Ma'am, where are you?"

"In the lounge Jack," she answered, raising her voice a little more than was necessary. Juliet appeared to have drifted away to a safer place, and Kelly knew she had to pull her back. It worked. Juliet sat up straight as Robson came in with three SOCO officers.

Kelly pointed to the back of the sofa and he walked round to take a look. "Oh Christ," he said. "Why did she do this? Just when we'd got Mountford …"

Kelly put up her hand to stop him. "We'll talk about all that back at the station, I think. When Professor Bailey has had chance to calm down."

"I'm perfectly calm," said Juliet. "Calm and relieved. All the waiting is over now." She turned to Kelly. "It's been the waiting that's been the hardest part. Waiting and not knowing. Now everything is clear."

Kelly sighed, rubbed her forehead and stood up. "Professor Juliet Bailey, I'm arresting you for the murder of Doctor Luke Thackray."

Juliet stood up obediently. Kelly took her by the arm and led her down the hallway towards the front door. Robson heard her voice fading. "You do not have to say anything but it may harm your defence …"

36

The summer had been long and warm, but it was now late September and Joseph could feel a damp chill in the air as he got out of his car. His left arm still pained him in some positions and the morning chill didn't help his leg, either. *But thank God for cars with automatic transmission.* He took the walking stick out from behind his seat and locked the car. He didn't really need the stick all the time now, but it still helped to have a little support as he climbed the few steps up to the science building.

He walked into his office to see the familiar sight of Mike sitting at his desk. He was wearing what had now become his trademark beanie hat, pulled down to cover what was left of the pinna of his right ear. He looked up. "Hi peg-leg."

Joseph smiled. "Hi Vincent. Welcome back to the asylum. Are Sophie and Johnny still doing well?" He hung the walking stick over the back of his chair and sat down, wincing at the discomfort in his left hip.

Mike smiled. "Yeah, great thanks. Johnny loves the cot mobile you got him last week. It gets him off to sleep like a charm." He stretched and leaned back in his chair. "I've really enjoyed paternity leave, but it's good to get back to work. We can start to settle into normal life again."

Joseph laughed. "With a small baby! I know what you mean though. After the last six months I'm yearning for the ordinary."

"There's still Juliet's trial to come, although I don't think it'll take very long," said Mike. "Seems open and shut."

"Well, the circumstances are pretty clear, but I think the sentence will hinge around the balance of her mind. She's been having psychiatric treatment since her arrest."

"Have you seen her much?" asked Mike.

"Once I was well enough to visit her on remand, yes. I've been a few times."

"What's your assessment of her, as a friend?"

Joseph hesitated. "Well, er, she's not the same person. It's weird, but that's the best way I can describe it. The old Juliet doesn't live there anymore. Egraine succeeded in destroying her too, in the end."

Mike winced at the mention of Egraine's name. "And it sounds like she destroyed DI Kelly's career too."

"Oh, I think her career could have survived Egraine's suicide and Thackray's murder, if she'd really wanted it to. From what little I heard from her, her resignation was something of a relief."

"Do you know what she's doing now?"

"Yes, gone into the forensic service. It's where she belongs, in my view."

Mike grinned. "She had a soft spot for you, methinks!"

Joseph grinned back, with a twinkle in his eye. "Yes, OK, Anna spotted that too. And if I'm honest, so did I. Between you and me, I quite enjoyed it for a while. I guess it played up to my waning middle-aged male ego." He suddenly looked crestfallen. "But I should have just acted my age and listened to her advice as a police officer, and then I wouldn't have two metal pins in my leg."

"Well at least you didn't behave like a total twat, like me."

Joseph lowered his voice. "Does Sophie know?"

"No. The police were happy to leave it with the explanation that Gary attacked me on Egraine's orders after I turned her down. Which is true. Essentially. I've wrestled with whether or not to tell Sophie what actually happened, but I think it would do more damage to tell her than not. Or maybe I'm just being a coward." He stood up and walked over to the window, taking up the customary thinking pose. "Or perhaps it's a bit of both."

Joseph got up slowly and limped over to stand by his friend. Mike turned to face him, a habit he had developed since the injury to his ear which had left him essentially deaf on his right side. Joseph saw the dampness in Mike's eyes. "I think enough people are suffering from the scars of this case. Even poor Nimue, all that time ago," Joseph said.

"I love Sophie and Johnny so much," said Mike. "I wouldn't hurt them for anything."

Joseph put his hand on his friend's shoulder as they both turned back to look out of the window. "You know, I've been thinking about what we could do to make something good come of all this."

"That would be a bloody miracle!" laughed Mike, sniffing and wiping his nose with the back of his hand. "What have you got in mind?"

Joseph limped back to his chair and sat down. "We should finish Watermark."

Mike turned around. "Did I hear you right? Alec's paper?"

Joseph took a deep breath, unsure about how Mike would react to his next revelation. "Well, according to Elaine Kelly, it was Egraine's."

"What?!"

"Egraine wrote it for Alec, to try to make the water-based theories of evolution more accepted. That's why she used Watermark as the main title, I guess. She wanted to make the point that we all carry one in our genes."

Mike chewed his lip. "Well, she was intelligent, there's no doubt about that. And it's a good paper. Or at least a good start." He came back to his desk and sat down heavily.

"I'd completely understand if you didn't want to touch it with a barge pole. But I do think we could make a contribution with it, even though it needs quite a bit more work. And that way Alec and Egraine would make a contribution too. They were both flawed people, that's for sure. But they did both have something important to say. We'd give them full attribution."

Mike nodded in agreement. "And we could give Nimue a voice too. In the short time I was working on her I couldn't help wondering what happened. She was definitely killed, murdered, I'm sure of that. We'll never know her story, but we can still learn from her."

Joseph raised his empty coffee mug. "Stick the kettle on and we'll drink to Nimue, then!"

37

It was evening. The sun began to set over the lake as Grandmother walked up to the top of a low hill and looked out over the water. Her daughter had been missing for three sunsets, and she instinctively knew that she was dead; knew that her daughter would never leave her children.

The lake had swallowed her.

Tears formed at the corners of her eyes and gently rolled down her face. *My girl in lake* she thought to herself.

It was important to say it. To let the thought out.

"Nim oo ee ay."

Appendix One

Watermark: the contribution of water to human evolution (latest draft)

Alec R Whickham, University of the North West of England, UK.

Abstract

Write later.

Introduction

Hypotheses defended by Hardy (1960), Morgan (1997) and others argue that an aquatic environment was the major causative agent in human evolution, following the final split from the chimpanzee/human most recent common ancestor. This paper argues that water did indeed play an important part in those evolutionary changes, but that it was a facilitator of them rather being the sole or main evolutionary imperative. This argument is developed through a synthesis of extant literatures drawn from archaeology, palaeontology and genetics, together with early findings from the analysis of remains excavated on the eastern shore of Lake Turkana, Kenya, of a *Homo ergaster* adult female who died approximately 1.5 million years ago (mya). The remains, which will be referred to in this paper as the Turkana Diving Female (TDF), were found in a position that is highly suggestive of immersion in several feet of water at the time of death. Fossilised fresh water mussels that were attached to the rock over which the fossils were found demonstrate that the rock was under enough water to enable colonisation by *Unionoida*.

There are many characteristics that differentiate *Homo sapiens* from other mammals but this paper will concentrate upon three of the main characteristics as a vehicle for discussion, viz.

- Locomotion, swimming and diving
- Brain development, language and communication
- Hair, skin and sweating

Locomotion, swimming and diving

The archaeological evidence appears to demonstrate that there were apes capable of walking upright at least 4.4 mya (White et al, 2009). Some authors (see, for example,*check bibliography*) argue that humans and chimpanzees might have had ancestors with very early tendencies to spend at least some of their time upright before the chimpanzee/human split 5-6 mya, based upon suggestive evidence from finds such as *Orrorin tugenensis* which are dated at around 6 mya. The human line continued to walk on two legs and to further hone the skill, whilst the chimpanzee line returned to the trees. Certainly, by 4.4 mya, species such as *Ardipithecus ramidus* were no longer suspending from branches or knuckle-walking and had both bipedal and so-called "careful climbing" adaptations. Dentition appears to show that *Ardipithecus* consumed a largely plant-based diet, and analysis of other animal specimens in the same strata as the *Ardipithecus* finds are indicative of a woodland environment, distant from large bodies of water (Louchart et al 2009).

It would appear, then, that early upright walking is unlikely to have been an adaptation to enable wading in an aquatic environment, or at least that upright walking can and did begin to develop away from large bodies of water. However, it can be argued that upright walking confers a significant advantage on apes that capitalise on water as a source of food, by conferring the ability to wade easily and therefore access to rich food sources such as fish and shellfish. This would be especially advantageous if other sources of food had become scarce. The location of the TDF finds, on top of an ancient shellfish bed, is strong evidence that early *Homo* species were, indeed, living in close proximity to shellfish. The long legs and gracile form of Homo ergaster also lends itself to wading and swimming. Wading in gradually deeper water may then have led to voluntary swimming and, ultimately, the ability to dive. Both of these abilities are much better developed in *Homo sapiens* than in any other of the great apes. It is notable that many examples of bipedal apes later than *Ardipithecus*, such as the *Australopithicines*, have been found in wet environments (WoldeGabriel et al, 2001).

Disagreements about what brought about the transit from "bent-knee walking" (which would have characterised the early attempts at upright walking by arboreal apes) to fully upright walking, have gone on for some time. Bent-knee walking is an inefficient method of locomotion relative to both quadripedal and modern human bipedal locomotion, and represents a transitional adaptation. So what would encourage a shift from spending some time walking upright with bent knees to specialising in bipedalism? Research into the relative energy costs of fully upright and bent-knee walking show that wading in both shallow and deeper water reduces the energy differential between them, and Kuliukas et al (2009) argue that it eases the energy/benefit controversy if wading through water is assumed to be one of the environmental selectors for upright walking.

Will we ever be able to firmly identify when bipedalism developed in human ancestors? Clues to the evolution of human characteristics can sometimes be gathered from examples of when individuals display non-typical characteristics. An example of this is Unertan Syndrome, where individuals walk on all fours to varying degrees. The existence and definition of this syndrome is still controversial, having been coined by Professor Uner Tan whilst at the Cukurova Medical School in Turkey (Tan, 2005). When this syndrome was first recognised, the quadripedalism exhibited by affected patients was accompanied by severe language deficiencies and a range of other mental disabilities. Since Tan's first paper, further examples of individuals who display quadripedalism have been identified; for example, two children who display upright walking but go onto all fours when they need to move rapidly (Tan & Tan, 2009). These children display no mental disability and have normal speech and cognitive abilities. Some patients affected by Unertan syndrome also sit awkwardly, in a manner that is reminiscent of how chimpanzees sit, with the head jutting forward rather than sitting vertically atop the spine. This syndrome, whilst very rare, appears to be inherited via the X chromosome and suggests that, in time, it may be possible to locate the gene or genes that affect bipedalism in the human genome and thereby shed some light on when it first developed in human ancestors.

So, the first contention of this paper is that as bipedalism was developing it enabled wading, and wading eased the transition from bent-knee to fully upright walking. Wading then led to swimming and, eventually, to diving, as a means of procuring food.

Brain development, language and communication

Probably the most defining difference between humans and other apes is brain size. The modern human brain has an average size of around 1300 - 1500 cc, more than three times the size of the average modern chimpanzee brain. The big question is why this rapid development occurred in humans whilst chimpanzee brains have hardly changed in size at all over the same period. What happened to human ancestors that didn't happen to chimpanzees after the split from the common ancestor? And why did the acceleration in brain size begin more than 2 million years after human ancestors were displaying bipedalism? If bipedalism was the instigating factor for brain development, why the delay before the rapid acceleration?

These questions lie at the heart of debates around the causation of human evolution. But before we discuss these, we need to understand what we mean by causation.

Deterministic vs stochastic causation.

Human evolution, and indeed any evolution, follows stochastic causation, i.e. that changes are more likely to occur in the presence of some environmental factors than their absence. The causation we are considering is not deterministic – we can't say that bipedalism caused brain development, or that water caused brain development. That is inappropriate terminology.

Burling (2005), in his book on the evolution of language, argues that all animals understand a range of gestures and calls that are innate in a species and require very little learning. Scowls, laughs and smiles are pretty well universal in human cultures and mean the same thing everywhere. Most animals display the ability to understand these types of gestures and calls, like a dog's tail between its legs, a wolf's howl, a bee's waggle dance or a tiger's flattened ears. But, what humans can do that no other animal can, is to agree on signs, symbols and sounds that enable the communication of ideas, feelings, beliefs – the list of what can be communicated is a long one. So, why? Why did humans develop sophisticated language ability and no other animal ever has? At least to date.

Burling gives us some interesting pointers to how and why accelerated brain development may have occurred in the way it did in humans. He argues that in much of the literature on the development of language, emphasis is placed on its production, i.e. making sounds, developing syntax and grammar, and so on. But logically, the ability to understand pre-language meaning from instrumental acts like pointing and other hand and body movements, is more likely to have evolved first. There is no point in making sounds, or indeed doing anything else, to convey meaning if the receiver is not equipped to understand that meaning. Communication requires an understanding receiver as much, if not more than, a skilled producer. Research into the capacity to understand language also shows that humans have the capacity to understand more than they can say. So, if comprehension needs to predate production, as Burling puts it "...what selective pressures could have driven our pre-human and early human ancestors towards interpreting the instrumental acts of other individuals?"

The answer is likely to be a stochastic (probabilistic) one. Or, more accurately, a combination of factors occurred together and each one made the development of that ability a bit more likely. Together those factors created the environment that made language development very likely. Chimps stayed in an environment that made it less likely.

In terms of selection, Burling (2005) suggests that

"... the human brain more than doubled its size in the last two million years, from less than 600 cc to more than 1200cc today, and yet technology, to the extent that it can be judged from stone tools, advanced hardly at all until the last tenth of that time. The brain had expanded nearly to its modern size before technology shows much sign of change. If we can see nothing to show for it in the archaeology, what in the world was all that brain expansion good for? One answer is that the brain was not being selected for technology at all, but for better music, language and humour, and for the kind of imagination that could invent religion and tell stories. In this case, new behaviour could have flowed with little noticeable impact on the surviving archaeological record. The pressures of both natural and sexual selection gave the most benefits to the individuals with the best social skills."

Selection for bigger brains must have begun with selection for pre-existing abilities that were beginning to develop in smaller brained ancestors. Around ten million years ago apes were the most intelligent animals on the planet, and it is therefore not surprising that modern humans evolved from them.

How a vocal language developed has also long been a point of discussion amongst language scholars. It seems that the adaptations that enable speech make the vocal tract of humans very different from those of the other great apes. It seems plausible that early language would have been gestural and visual, so then why would it have given way to a vocal language? As Burling says;

"A speculative answer, but an answer that we should probably take seriously, is to propose that voluntary control over the vocal tract came first as an adaptation to something other than language."

What might be that adaptation? Burling argues that it might be for singing and chanting, but Morgan (1990) argues that it was due to our ancestors living in water and selecting for the ability to hold the breath for swimming and diving. That resulted in a shift in the position of the larynx, and the ability to consciously control our breathing, which in turn gave Homo sapiens the ability to begin making speech sounds. Further adaptations then produced more control over the tongue and lips so that a greater range of sounds could be made, with a constant selection bias for better and better socialisation and communication. These are the situations that make language more likely to develop than not, and also account for the rapid acceleration in brain development over the past 2 million years.

Language is generally perceived as being a tremendous benefit to our species, and indeed it is in many ways. But, all things come at a price. The developments that are necessary in the brain to enable speech also means that humans suffer from a unique range of mental disabilities like autism and schizophrenia (see, for example, Crow 2000). Research has shown that schizophrenia manifests itself in the same way in all cultures, from aboriginal Australian people to Inuit Eskimos and from Javanese to Germans (Kraepelin 1920, Murphy 1976, Mowry et al 1994). It appears to be a basic human trait, and it is therefore at least possible that it was manifest in some form in our earlier ancestors as the brain developed. If we consider Burlings' hypothesis that language could have developed gradually over a time period of millions of years, then it is likely that some of the mental dysfunctions that modern humans suffer developed alongside it. Language must, therefore, have conferred a significant advantage to make it worth the disabilities that accompany it.

*Note: expand this quite a bit

Hair, skin and sweating

Why pubic hair? And facial hair? And armpit hair? And why does the hair on our head keep growing? It is often written that humans are "naked", but this is not the case. It is rather that our covering of hair has adapted very specifically relative to the other great apes, reducing in length and density on many parts of our body, but becoming bushier and denser, or growing much longer, on other parts. Why this happened is a question that has many hypotheses put forward to explain it. When it happened may be an easier question to try to answer, but as usual the possible explanations diverge in both timing and cause.

The biological theories consider the evolution of parasites as one clue to the changing hair patterns of ancestors of Homo sapiens. Louse species that specialise in modern human infestation are of three types; hair and body lice of the genus *Pediculus*, and pubic (or "crab") lice of the genus *Phthiris*. The fact that humans are host to three different types of lice is unusual in itself, as most species have just one, specialised louse. Even more strangely, the *Pediculus* louse is related to the chimpanzee louse, but *Phthirus* is related to the gorilla louse. By comparing the DNA of the human pubic louse and the modern gorilla louse, Reed et al (*check the date for this one*) have demonstrated that the split between the two louse species took place around 3.3 million years ago, suggesting that for some reason, human ancestors became re-infested with the gorilla louse some time before that and made a final split from gorilla contact 3.3 mya. How this might have happened is open to wide speculation, from sexual contact that resulted in some re-hybridisation of human ancestors prior to 3.3 mya, through to picking up stray lice that had fallen onto beds when human ancestors used old gorilla beds for sleeping.

However, the fact that chimpanzees and the other great apes did not become re-infested with gorilla lice does suggest some kind of special contact between gorillas and proto-human species. It also suggests that proto-human species possessed hair that was both like the gorilla and like the chimpanzee prior to 3.3 mya, as the species was infested by both types of louse.

Notes:
Need to round these arguments up and say what it all means.

Check for errors and expand bibliography. Some refs need work. Add refs list.

A?

Bibliography

A.S. (1634). *Panolbion, or, The Blessednes of the Saints*. London: Printed for William Sheares. Available electronically from the National Library of Australia at http://catalogue.nla.gov.au/Record/3443427 . Original in Emmanuel College Library, University of Cambridge, U.K.

Burling R. (2007). *The Talking Ape*. Oxford: Oxford University Press.

Crow T.J. (2000). Schizophrenia as the price that Homo sapiens pays for language: a resolution of the central paradox in the origin of species. *Brain Research Reviews*, vol 31, issues 2-3, pp. 118-129.

Kuliukas A.V., Milne N. & Fournier P. (2009). The relative cost of bent-knee walking is reduced in water. *Journal of Comparative Human Biology*, Vol 60, pp. 479-488.

Morgan E. (1990). *The Scars of Evolution*. Oxford: Oxford University Press.

Morgan E. (1997). *The Aquatic Ape Hypothesis*. London: Souvenir Press.

Morgan E. (1985). *The Descent of Woman*. London: Souvenir Press. 2nd edition.

Morgan E. (2008). *The Naked Darwinist*. Eildon Press.

Patterson N., Richter D.J., Gnerre S., Lander E.S. & Reich D. (2006). Genetic evidence for complex speciation of humans and chimpanzees. *Nature*, vol 441, pp. 1103 – 1108.

Pollard K.S. (2009). What makes us human? *Scientific American*, May 2009.

Reed D.L., Smith V.S., Hammond S.L., Rogers A.R. & Clayton D.H. (2004). Genetic analysis of lice supports direct contact between modern and archaic humans. *PLoS Biol*, vol 2, number 11.

Shubin N. (2007). *Your Inner Fish*. London: Penguin.

Tan U. (2005). Unertan Syndrome: quadrupedality, primitive language and severe mental retardation. *NeuroQuantology*, issue 4, pp. 250-255.

Tan U. & Tan M. (2009). A new variant of Unertan Syndrome: running on all fours in two upright-walking children. *International Journal of Neuroscience*, vol 119, number 7, pp.909-918.

Verhaegen M., Puech P-F & Munro S. (2002). Aquarboreal ancestors? *Trends in Ecology and Evolution*, Vol 17, issue 5, pp. 212-217.

Wade N. (2007). In lice, clues to human origin and attire. *New York Times*, 8th March 2007.

Wade N. (2007). *Before the Dawn: recovering the lost history of our ancestors*. London: Duckworth.

White T., Asfaw B., Beyene Y., Haile-Selassie Y., Lovejoy C.O., Suwa G. & WoldeGabriel G. (2009). Ardipithecus ramidus and the paleobiology of early hominids. *Science*, vol 326, number 5949, pp. 64, 75-86.

Ziaee A.A. (2010). Islamic Cosmology and Astronomy: *Ibrahim Hakki's Marifetname*. LAP LAMBERT Academic Publishing.